TRACKS

Also by Clayton Bess

Story for a Black Night
The Truth About the Moon
Big Man and the Burn-Out

TRACKS

Clayton Bess

Houghton Mifflin Company
Boston 1986

Library of Congress Cataloging in Publication Data

Bess, Clayton.
  Tracks.

  Summary: Two restless brothers, Monroe and Blue,
learn quickly about life and the nature of people while
following the railroad tracks in the Southwest during
the Depression.
    [1. Depressions—1929—Fiction. 2. Southwest, New—
Fiction. 3. Voyages and travels—Fiction. 4. Brothers—
Fiction] I. Title.
  PZ7.B4654Tp 1986   [Fic]   85-27349
  ISBN 0-395-40571-8

Printed in the United States of America

P 10 9 8 7 6 5 4 3 2 1

For my families,
the Lockes, the Holts, and the Johnsons,
but most especially for
Blue and Marge — Clay and Bess.

This story was told to me and my friend
Meechum by my grandpa, Sid Roan. I wrote it
down just the way he told it. Or pretty much.
                              Jess Judd

TRACKS

One

IT WAS BLISTERING HOT the day I hopped my first freight. Heat rays waved up off those tracks, and I about went blind from eyeburn waiting for that train to start up. Outside of laying dead in your grave, there ain't nothing in this world so purely poisonous dull as watching a setting train.

But once that train starts to roll, watch out. It comes rumbling down on you like a mountain on skis. And my, if it ain't just thrilling!

Now, I told you already the way the tracks was set up in Atoka, Oklahoma, running south to north, stretching away just as far as the eye could see, the wood crossties repeating themselves till the mind boggled. I sat there on a crouch trying to count them, but no good.

Monroe, I knowed, would make his jump first. I had already hunted him up, spied him first thing hiding out with a couple of hoboes in a stand of post oaks just off the right of way. Knowing that if Monroe found me hanging around he'd see what I was up to and send me home with a bootprint on my tail, I snuck further out. I found me a culvert growed around with prairie grass a hundred yards or so north of him, and ducked into it to wait.

And now at last, here the train starts up, headed north, making that lazy *bump-bump-bump* as the couplings engage. The engine noses out of the yard, then starts picking up speed. As soon as it gets past the stand of post oaks, and the boxcars come filing by, the two hoboes break from their cover, running alongside the train until they pick out an empty boxcar and swing theirselves in. Monroe, he follows suit, catching onto the hasp of the boxcar door and hoisting hisself up and swiveling his backside in to sit flat down on the floor just as easy as if he was home in Mama's rocking chair.

By this time the car's drawing alongside my culvert and I peeks out over the grass and stares up and right into Monroe's eyes. I can tell that at first he don't see what he's seeing, but just thinks I'm some kid hanging around the train yard. Then he recognizes me. His mouth drops open and his hand shoots up in a wave. I know it's now or never. He's not leaving me behind, not again.

I jumps out of the culvert and shins after him. He yells, and even though the noise of the train drowns him out, I knows well enough what he's saying. But I gots a train to catch, so I just puts my head down and runs.

The train's picking up speed all the time, and if I had the sense God give a goose, I'd see I'm a little short in the pants, and I'd give it up. Even a full-growed man would think twice't about grabbing onto a freight going this fast, and I'm just a kid, and a runt at that. But they say the Lord protects fools, drunks, and kids, and I guess it's true or I'd be sitting here today dead.

2

Now, I'm ten years old at this time, and Monroe must be seventeen. No, I'm eleven, and the year is 19 and 34, and I'll tell you how I know. My Mama just bought me a new pair of shoes for my eleventh birthday, little dress-up shoes for church, don't you know, a real luxury item in those days cause those was hard times. Never before had I owned a true and proper pair but wore only pinchy, holey hand-me-downs. Or better, went barefoot. But it was Mama's wedding again, her first one in church, and she didn't want her kids shaming her in front of her new husband, so she bought me them shoes.

And I've got them on now, and I can see them down there pumping away under me as I runs, and I tell you they're earning their price today. Them sharp rocks in the ballast is cutting up that leather like it's paper. I'm a sprinter, and fast too, and I pretty easy pulls even with the door of Monroe's boxcar. He squats down and yells into my ear.

"You gone get killed!"

"I'm coming with you!" I yells back, or tries to. But I don't know if I gets any of it out, cause I needs all my breath for running. I reaches up to him for a hand-up, but he folds his arms across his chest and stands back.

"Huh-uh," he yells. "You get home!"

Now the train starts gaining on me, picking up real speed while me, I starts to give out. The back edge of the door comes even with me. I holds onto the frame for a second but loses it. I sees the door hasp up above me and thinks about jumping for it like I seen Monroe do, but it's pretty high up there, and I chickens out. Up ahead I sees the wheels churning along and I can hear more of

3

them at my side, and more behind me. I remembers the dead man me and my friend Marge found on the tracks the other side of town, his head severed clean off his body and throwed fifty foot away, his eyes wide and staring like he was saying, "Who, me?"

Yes, and it could be me, too, in about two seconds if I don't watch out.

My hand brushes the wall of the boxcar as it slides by me, leaving me behind. I sees Monroe's face as he leans out the door to watch, still shouting and waving me off the roadbed. Then I feels a steel bar under my fingers. It's the bottom rung of the ladder at the end of the boxcar. I'm making up my mind to clamp down on it when the ballast gives under me and my ankle turns and I starts to fall. I sees that track coming up at my face and hears the grind and clack of that wheel just behind my ear and I heaves myself upright, saying, "Not yet," still running just like an idiot.

But I've lost my opportunity to grab that ladder. Now, later on I finds out from the boes that this was lucky for me. You see, when catching a freight you don't never want to grab onto the rear ladder of a boxcar, not if the train's moving any speed at all, cause the train throws you back into the coupling gap between the cars, which breaks your grip and drops you under the wheels. No, what you want to do is catch the ladder on the front of the car; then when the train throws you up, you hit against the wall of the car and it protects you while you climb the ladder and secure yourself a berth.

So that's what I do, accidental, as I say, because of turning my ankle. While I'm stumbling along there trying to

4

regain my balance, the next car pulls alongside and my hand hits that ladder rung at the front of the car and my fingers curls around it, and before I knows it my feet is out from under me and I'm attached to the train, just flapping like a flag in the wind up against that boxcar, going sixty down those tracks.

And there I freezes. I just don't got the mental where-withal to figure what to do now. I guess my eyes is wide staring open, though, cause I sees what happens next like it's a movie playing on a screen before me.

I sees Monroe leaning out the door of his car, and behind him the heads of the two boes. The looks on their faces, ghastly white and drawn about a foot long, lets me know the kind of trouble I'm in if I don't have the sense to see it myself. Seeing me froze there on that bottom rung, not even making an effort to climb the ladder, they goes into a huddle and starts looking around them. Monroe disappears into the boxcar a minute, and when he comes back he's got in his hand a hay hook and a length of rope. You see, they had chose theirselves a car that had transported hay the last time out, because that way they could make theirselves a little pallet out of the scattered hay. And this hay hook and lashing rope was left behind by some swamper, too sleepy or careless to finish cleaning up. You tell me He didn't have his eye on the sparrow that day!

Monroe ties the rope onto the handle of the hook, all the while glancing back at me to see if I'm still a passenger. Then he gets the two boes to hang onto him and he leans way out the door, looking up, and swings that rope with the hook and lets it fly up and over the car. At first I

5

don't see what he's up to. All I see is that hook come clattering down the roof of that car and drop into the coupling gap, coming within an inch or two of parking its point in my head. I about lose my grip, and decide I'd be better off with my eyes closed. So I closes them. My arms is starting to wear out now. They was about ripped out of their sockets when I grabbed onto the train, and now they're feeling like tubes of glass stretched out in front of me, liable to just shatter any second.

I hears a noise and opens up my eyes. Monroe, he's thrown the hay hook again, and this time it has looped up over the roof of the car and caught up under the other side of the catwalk. The catwalk is the walkway on top of the train that the brakemen and bulls use to get from one end of the train to the other, a narrow, raised platform of slats that runs the length of every car.

I sees now what Monroe's up to. He tests the rope to see if the hook will hold, then he takes hisself a big breath and swings out the door and starts walking up the side of the boxcar. Now I never seen this done before nor since, but I guess without a fool kid brother like me, it has never been necessary before nor since.

Monroe clambers onto the catwalk and stands up in a crouch. The train now is hitting its peak speed, just going lickety brindle, rocking and bucking like a wild horse, no place to be on the top of. He makes his way to the back of the car and jumps the gap to my car and climbs down the ladder to me. He loosens his belt, which is just an old hank of rope, and ties hisself by the waist onto the ladder. Then he bends down and holds out a hand to me.

6

Now my fingers is clenched so tight around that steel rung that for the life of me I can't open them up to catch aholt of Monroe's hand. Seems like I'm welded to that boxcar. So Monroe, he grabs onto my forearm and gives me a mighty jerk loose and hauls me quick up into his arms. I puts my face into his chest and just bawls like a baby.

And truth to tell, I guess I'm not much more than a baby at this time. Eleven years old and facing death. But that doesn't take away the sting of breaking down like that in front of Monroe.

And we ain't out of it yet. We still have to get inside the other car.

"Can you climb?" Monroe yells.

I don't think I can. My arms and legs is no better than rubber now. But I nods yes, all the same, feeling ashamed and just generally foolish and feeble.

Monroe sizes me up, though, and knows I'm all gone. He unties hisself from the ladder and loops the rope around me and then reties it around his waist so I'm tied onto him. Then he climbs the ladder, dragging me up with him, until he gets us onto the catwalk where we rests for a minute, laying crumpled up, holding onto the slats.

I looks over to the catwalk of the next car and tries not to think what happens next. We gots to jump, I knows that, but it don't look possible. That car over there is lunging and heaving, but not any way like our car is. It bucks up and we drops down; it rolls right and we rolls left. I wonders to myself how Monroe is ever going to manage with me tied on him.

7

"You're going to have to jump on your own!" Monroe yells, and I starts feeling sick. That's when I notices for the first time that I have messed my pants.

Now I know you've heard the expression, and it's true. You face something scary enough and that old sphincter muscle just opens wide and spews. And you do, you get it scared right out of you.

So here's me and Monroe and a pantsful of it up on top of that train. I figures Monroe must know about my accident too, cause here he is leaning right over me to untie me. But he don't sniff nor let on. Then before I knows it, he crouches and leaps and then there he is over there on that catwalk and me still back over here. "Come on!" he shouts. "I'll catch you."

Well, by this time I'm ready to die anyway of fear and shame, and I don't even give it another thought but I swallows my heart and throws myself through the air and, to my surprise, lands like a cat beside Monroe. He grabs me, but it's not necessary cause I've got my fingers wrapped around those slats, and I'm not going noplace. I sees a light in Monroe's eyes, and I knows I come back up a notch in his esteem. I starts feeling a little better myself. Fact of business, it begins to seem a little like fun.

We crawls along the catwalk to where the hay hook is still catched up under the slats, and we makes ready to climb down the rope into the boxcar. Monroe starts to loosen his belt to tie me back onto him, but by this time I'm starting to feel right big again.

"I can climb down myself!" I yells.

"Bull!" Monroe yells back and ties me on. Then he grabs aholt the rope and slips over the side of the car. I looks down at them rocks flying by below and I gets dizzy and glad Monroe had the sense to tie me up.

When we gets down alongside the doorway, the boes is right there with a hand to pull us inside. Finally we're safe.

First thing Monroe does when he gets me untied is turn me around and slap me upside the head so hard I see stars. Then he hugs me to him and bawls, too.

I guess Monroe, he ain't much more than a baby either. I guess none of us is, ever.

Two

A LOT OF YEARS is gone now, but I still remember every-thing about that first day out. Everything. Well, it's not the kind of thing you do forget, sitting in an old straw-blowing boxcar trying to clean up a pair of messy jeans.

I found me a corner of the car and sat down by myself to do it. And it wasn't at all pleasant. Monroe and the boes sat in the doorway looking out, giving me as much privacy as you can have, four in a boxcar.

In those days they used to line boxcars with a good, heavy, feltlike paper — maybe they still do; I don't know — and using the short blade on my Barlow I stripped off some of that. It cleaned up the skin pretty well, as good as toilet paper today would, but I knowed I'd need soap and water to get my pants clean.

I come back to the doorway and sat with Monroe and the boes, downwind of course. Some boes could get pretty ripe when they'd been on the road awhile without seeing water, but nobody was nothing next to me. They wrinkled their noses and pulled back a ways, but they didn't get right up and leave, so I figured I was passable.

Monroe said, "This is Earl and that's Bosco Pete. This here's my kid brother, Blue."

Now I guess I should explain right off why they called me Blue when I was a kid. My real name, as you know, is Sid, or Sidney really, named after the town where my father was from. My full name is Sidney Australia Roan, which my Mama said made me sound like an emperor, but which I could never get wholly behind. Mama had a real flair for naming her kids, relying solely on whim and circumstance. That's why my older sister, born on Christmas day, was named Gloria Excelsior; and the next sister, born within the year while Mama was visiting Aunt Clemmy down in Janetville, Texas, was named after a picture book of kings and queens Mama found laying on the coffee table and which she was thumbing through just before she hit the bed with Janet Plantagenet.

Now Gloria Excelsior and Janet Plantagenet was both by Mama's second husband, Grover Hoyle, or as Mama always referred to him, the no-good Mr. Hoyle. My father come a year later, and he was the no-good Mr. Roan. I never knowed either of them because the no-good Mr. Hoyle died of the dropsy while Mama was pregnant with Janet Plantagenet, and the no-good Mr. Roan got drunk the night I was born and fell in Boggy Crick just outside Atoka and got drownded.

Mama never loved but one of her husbands, and that was the first one, Steven Monroe, and she loved him to distraction. He loved her back, too, and they did everything for each other, couldn't stand being away from each other for even so long as a quarter of an hour, just full of each other. Mama was so full of him that when their first

11

child was born, she called the boy every name after the father, Monroe Monroe Monroe. When Monroe got big, he shortened it to Monroe M. Monroe, but there wasn't nobody who didn't know what the M. stood for.

When the First World War come along Steven Monroe was called away to the army, and he never come back, but was shot through the heart with a German bullet. I guess Mama went about crazy, to hear Aunt Clemmy tell of it. Mama never mentioned his name again, except it was referring to Monroe the son.

It was no wonder then, heartbroken as she was, that Mama went to the no-goods. My father wasn't the last of them, either. After him come a man I myself remember, a dark, pointy-nosed man by the name Samuel Grayson who fathered a child with Mama that I believe was born out of wedlock. In any case I don't recall either a marriage or a divorce, and the no-good Mr. Grayson wasn't around long. The baby was poorly for months, and so was Mama. She never even named him, knowing he wasn't long for the world, but just called him "the baby" so as not to get too close to him and break her heart again. Just before he reached his ebb, Mama called out the Holiness preacher, who sprinkled some baptismal water on the baby to save his soul. He told her she'd best name the baby so as to find him in heaven when she got there too, but she couldn't think of anything. So I called him Tom, and he died.

For my part, I was born early. Mama wasn't looking for me for weeks, and she says that's why I turned out so runty. She was out in the fields picking cotton and wasn't halfway through her first bag when I come on. I guess I come on fast, too, cause she couldn't get home but just laid down between the rows and give me up. Her head rolling in the dirt, all she could see was all that blue sky above, so she called me Blue, and the name stuck.

"How do, Blue?" said Earl.

"How do?" said Bosco Pete.

"How do?" I said back, and twisted away just a little as the wind gusted through the boxcar doorway in a new and compromising direction. Earl and Bosco Pete held their breaths and scooted across the car and slid open the other door. I looked down at my feet. There wasn't hardly nothing left of my new shoes.

"Mama'll cry when she sees them shoes," Monroe said. "It like to bust her to buy them."

"Well, she ain't gonna see them," I said. "So don't worry."

"You think you're mighty smart, Blue, cause you ain't dead?"

"No."

"Just where did you think you was heading?"

"With you."

He snorted.

"You know where I'm going, don't you? You think I want a kid with me?"

"I don't care," I said. "You got one."

"Does Mama know where you are?"

"No."

He snorted again. "Soon's we get to McAlester, we're turning right back, you hear?"

Now I snorted.

He cuffed me a good one on the left ear. "You got no care for no one but yourself, do you? What's Mama gonna say when she goes out looking for you and you're no-where? How's she gonna feel, wondering if you're lost or kidnapped or better yet kilt?"

"I left her a letter with Tad Daily," I said. "He's going to give it to her at sundown."

He said, "And just what kind of letter when you know you can't write?"

I said, "I guess I can write 'good-bye.' I guess I can sign my name."

I was growing pretty mad by this time because I didn't take to being goaded. It was true enough that I wasn't much for writing. It's still true. Oh, I can read a little and write a few words, but if someone's watching me or look-ing over my shoulder, I'm lucky to sign my name without a mistake. Monroe knowed this very well.

School was never for me. I just couldn't seem to catch on, somehow, got my letters all wrong and backwards, so all the kids laughed. Now, in arithmetic I was a whiz. I remember one day just astounding the class when a mile-long train went by with me totting up the serial numbers on the boxcars as they passed. Miss Hudson said I just made up my figures, but I didn't. It was a fair sum.

I remember looking forward to the fourth grade cause that's when you got your geography, and it was this grand book, great big and flat so you could stack all your other books on it nice and neat and sling them across your hip and just strut home from school. But I give it up in the third grade, wore out with trying, and Mama didn't make me go no more. So I never did get my geography. There just wasn't any sense in trying when I couldn't get my letters right. And runty as I was, I was the biggest kid in class from being held back so many times. Monroe, he used to joke that I was the only kid in grade school to get throwed out for not shaving.

I don't know, maybe I should have tried harder. Maybe I'd have done something. But here I was with Monroe, and here I was going to stay.

The train ride was awful lonesome. Monroe didn't say no more to me for the rest of the trip, but crossed the car and sat over there with Earl and Bosco Pete, keeping his back to me. I watched out the door as the countryside slipped by, all silent and empty. Off to the east lay the Jackfork Mountains looking hard against the sky. Every so often you'd see a house, or a little settlement growed up by the tracks, which showed there was a coal mine somewhere in the vicinity. A little kid seen me where he was playing in the mud his Mama made, splashing water as she drawed it from the well. He waved and I waved back. But I ain't never been so lonely as those hours on that first freight.

It was growing dark when we pulled into McAlester, where the westbound Rock Island Line crossed our tracks. I had never been to a big town before, so I just gawked. There was a hotel there that had six stories. And up on a hill was the new Masonic Temple, just glorious, and all lit up. Off to the north was the tallest standpipe I ever seen or imagined, a great big concrete reservoir, must have held a lakeful of water.

The train slowed down and Monroe and Earl and Bosco Pete stood up. So did I. They shook hands.

"Good luck to you," Bosco Pete said to Earl. "If there's work up there, you send word back."

Earl nodded and turned to Monroe. "And good luck to you, young feller," he said. "And if she's worth the finding, you'll find her, I guess."

Monroe answered, "She's worth it. You take care now."

Then Monroe turned to me. "Come on, Blue. We're getting off here."

Bosco Pete made the jump first, hitting the ground running. By this time the train was going only about five mile an hour, and he didn't have any trouble. Monroe jumped next, and then, running alongside the train, he held out his hand to me.

I yelled, "You get out of my way! I'm coming out on my own!"

Monroe stopped and put his hands on his hips and yelled, "Okay, Mr. Smart Alec, you just come ahead then!"

I turned to Earl and stuck out my hand. He took it and grinned and said, "You keep after him, kid. You do just fine."

Then I crossed to the door and took a measure of the ground. It looked mighty far down, and the ballast looked mighty rough, but I jumped. I hit the ground more on a stumble than on a run, but I pulled upright and pranced around back to Monroe. He turned away, but not so fast I didn't see the grin on his face.

"We'll wait here," he said, "for the next train back to Atoka."

I said, "No, we won't. We're going west."

He said, "You hesh your mouth before I hesh it for you."

He followed Bosco Pete, and I followed them both to a

16

sprawling brick building just off the right of way. An old sign said JOHNSON'S RUBBER FACTORY, but it hung askew and the paint was mostly peeled off, and I seen at once that the business was a casualty of the Depression. Through the broken windows I could see the lights of a few candles burning.

The door stood open, dragging on its hinges, and we went inside. It was dark and smelled of damp and rot. The building was honeycombed with little rooms divided by walls of cardboard or canvas hung from the rafters, and inside every room was a person or two, or a family. They looked up at us as we passed their cells, and their eyes was dull. One man and woman sat close together without looking up. She had a baby in her arms and the top of her dress open to give it her breast. But it wasn't suckling, and I don't think it was asleep neither. I think it was dead.

Now, we was always poor in our family, but Mama always managed to make us a home. These people had lost their homes, uprooted by the Depression and blowing over the land to find shelter and food wherever they could. Reports of them had drifted down to us in Atoka, and we seen that the boes riding the freights was getting more and more plentiful. But Atoka was a small town and no attraction for the homeless, so these was the first real Depression refugees I had seen.

I had heard of the Depression, of course, and had some idea what it meant, but not really. It's like people telling you about the ocean; you just have no idea until you see it. And even standing there looking at it, it's still too big to grasp. I knowed there had been what they called a Crash in New York in 19 and 29, and people killed themselves because it was so dreadful. But what was that to us in Atoka? We just kept living. Until little by little we started to feel it, too.

I remember Monroe had this little Model T Ford, and it was something. Well, it was nothing really, just an engine and a frame. Didn't have a hood, didn't have a windshield, didn't even have a seat, but you had to sit on the gas tank. If you had a little hill in front of you, you had to turn around and back up it. Otherwise the gas drained out of the engine, and it stalled. Oh, it was a dandy little automobile. Monroe drove it all over the countryside, and when I could give Mama the slip, he'd take me with him.

He was courting the Holiness preacher's twin daughters, so like as not you'd find us driving to a rendezvous over to the churchhouse. I was supposed to be the lookout. But the preacher, a big, swollen, bass-voiced man by the name Clyde Starr, had an eye like an eagle and he'd spy our dust and be at the bend waiting for us.

"Praise the Lord," he'd say when we rounded the bend, "for He has sent me His servants!" Then he'd enlist us into what he called "the service of God," building pews or adding a Sunday school room onto the chapel. Or if God's work was done, he'd put us to what Monroe called "the service of Starr," chopping wood or clearing land.

One night when we come home late, Mama give us a tongue-lashing. "You been to that church again! I told you to keep from there!"

"Why, it's for our souls, Mama!" Monroe said.

"The soles of my feet!" she said. "You been chasing that Starr girl."

"Which one, Mama?" I said. Monroe give me a kick under the table.

The real squeeze of the Depression started in earnest around 19 and 32. Monroe had to sell that dandy little Model T. We couldn't afford the gas for it anyway. It was nine cent a gallon, or maybe eight cent if they got a gas war going. But when you worked all day picking in the cotton fields at a penny a pound — and in these times, cotton in Oklahoma was awful poor and scraggly, and a good picker was lucky to get a hundred pounds in a long day, breaking your back, scabbing your knees, cutting up your fingers on the cusp of them bolls — nine cent for a ride to the churchhouse looked mighty steep.

After the Model T went Mama's buggy, and after the buggy her bay mare Maude. Then there wasn't nothing left on the place but food or food animals, and we needed them to eat. That's when Monroe started going afield to find work. Up north of McAlester he got a job riding line for Gulf Oil, checking for leaks in their pipelines stretching off east to the refineries in Pennsylvania.

About this time, things at home eased up for us a little because Gloria Excelsior and Janet Plantagenet got married. The Blake brothers from Monett, Missouri, passing through Atoka on their way home from the oil fields of Dallas, spied the girls window-shopping in front of Milady's Millinery Shoppe on Main Street. Gloria Excelsior had just turned fifteen and Janet Plantagenet was only fourteen, but girls married young those days. They was both of good stock, as filled out as a growed woman, and pretty enough to turn the head. David and Patrick Blake loitered around town three days, pestering first the girls, then Mama, for their hands in marriage, until finally, with a lot of push from the girls, Mama give in.

She said to Gloria Excelsior, "Well, I say yes, but I don't like it. Those boys are Catholic, and I wanted you to marry a Christian."

"Why, Mama, a Catholic's a Christian!"

"No!"

"Sure it is."

"Why do they call it a Catholic for, then?"

"Well, look here, Mama, you call yourself a Baptist, don't you?"

"I certainly do."

"Yet you're a Christian, aren't you?"

"I certainly am."

"Well?" Gloria Excelsior turned, triumphant, and went off with Janet Plantagenet to pack what duds they had. In a few minutes Mama looked them up.

"Now look here," Mama said. "Didn't those boys make you promise to bring up your children as a Catholic?"

"Yes," Gloria Excelsior said.

"And we did promise," Janet Plantagenet said.

"Which means you have renounced your own religion, which is Baptist, which is Christian. So you girls go ahead and marry your Catholic boys if you're bound on it, but don't go trying to tell me they're Christian. I'm not stupid!"

Gloria Excelsior and Janet Plantagenet married and went off to Monett, and though I have never seen them again, we have kept in touch through the years and I know that the Blake brothers made them happy. But that's another story.

Monroe, he done pretty good at first with Gulf Oil. He was a good worker, and bright, and after riding line a half year or so, they give him an inside job as a pumper, maintaining the big pumps. He started to teach hisself telegraphy, figuring to get promoted within the company. Any time he come home for a visit, you could see him with a pencil in his hand tapping out Morse code on the tabletop for practice.

But times was hard for the oil companies too, and Monroe got laid off. The whole country was in a tailspin. No money to buy nothing, which meant companies laid off their workers or went out of business, which meant the people didn't have money to buy nothing. What they call a vicious circle.

So Monroe started riding the freights, trying to find work. He heard they was thrashing wheat in Kansas, and off he went, disappearing north on the M, K & T, or Katy as we called her, the Missouri, Kansas & Texas Railway, which was the very line I told you about that we hopped to McAlester. And then, some days later, back he'd come. Maybe he got a day's work out of it, maybe he didn't. Then he heard they was taking on miners in the coal mines south of us, and back on old Katy. He took her all the way down to the Red River, which is the river that divides Oklahoma from Texas to the south. But back he come. Seemed like for every job, there was fifty men in line.

Around Atoka I could get work sometimes working as a waterjack on the railroad crews or piling brush for a farmer clearing land. But farmers wasn't clearing land much these times because there was no market for their crops. We kept a garden for vegetables for the dinner table, and we had hens laying, and a good milk cow, so we wasn't in danger of starving, but there was precious little in the way of extra. Mama made a few coins selling milk and eggs, but she was as likely to give it away as sell it just as soon as someone hungry looked her in the eye.

She started looking poorly, kindly thin, kindly pale-eyed. She was still a young woman by today's standards, but she had done a lot of living, bearing five kids and putting three men in their graves. She needed a rest.

And then along come Abe Boone.

Actually, Abe had been there all along, right there in Daisy, not fifteen mile as the crow flies from Atoka. That is, when the crow's not drunk. Seems the good Mr. Boone knowed Mama from when they was kids in school, when he was just crazy for her. But she had her heart bound up with Steven Monroe and married him, as I told you, and there was Abe left alone. So he found hisself a wife, a Christian Science woman named Ruth. That's all I know about her except that she died in childbirth in 19 and 33, delivering up their fifth living child, another boy. Abe spent one entire year in mourning for Ruth, and then he come looking for Mama, saying his boys needed a good mother and he needed a wife, and would she have him.

He had kept track of Mama through all the years and knowed about all the no-goods that followed Steven Monroe, but this had not dimmed the love he had always kept for her. Ruth had been a good, strong, loving wife, and he was content he had been a good husband, but he had never given his love to any woman because it belonged to only one woman, my Mama.

I did everything I could to keep Mama away from Abe, but she was too strong for me. She explained to me something I have puzzled over through all these many years since, the difference between gravity and fire.

"With the one," she told me, "you fall down, heavy and broken and no good for nothing in this world but breathing your last in the dirt. With the other, you burn up."

Now Mama wasn't never keen with words, no more than me. But I think I got an idea what she meant underneath her talk. I think she meant she loved Abe back, that his kind of love was good. So I swallowed down my jealousy, and I forced myself to stand up for her at the wedding and give her away. Monroe, he was there, too, and should rightfully have been the one to do it since he was Mama's first-born. But I think Mama knowed how lost I felt over losing her, and so she gave the honor to me.

"Lula," Abe said to Mama after it was over and all the A-mens said, "I told you twenty years ago that I would dance at your wedding with a cowbell on." Then Reg, Abe's oldest boy, he brought a cowbell on a blue satin ribbon and slipped it over Abe's head, and Abe did a jig before the whole congregation, and Mama joined him. I guess I never did see roses in her cheeks before, but they was there that day.

"Lula," Abe said when they stopped and he took her in his arms, "in my life you will be first, even before me."

He was a good man.

Three

Now I TOLD YOU about the Starr twins that Monroe was cute on. Well, we called them twins because they was the same age, but Rose Jewel and Marguerite Pearl was about as different as any two girls could be.

Rose Jewel was the elder by just fifteen minute, and she come out of the womb worldly wise. She was just as plump as a guinea hen and twice as flighty, with a spark in her eye that led more than one boy into the bushes after her, and Monroe was no exception. Her cheeks was always rosy, though I suspected she had help from a bottle, and her hair was a soft brown that burnished in the sunlight and just dazzled you. She had legs that wasn't meant for nothing but laying down.

Marguerite Pearl, or Marge as we all called her, had the legs of a horse, straight, strong, galloping legs. In fact Marge was horsy all over. Her face was the longest I ever seen on a girl, with a high forehead and a low, deep-clefted chin, and hollow cheeks under a pair of brown, glittery eyes set so wide apart in her head that she looked like she was watching the walls. Her hair was long and thick and so black it verged on blue. Mama called her Cheequaola, which I think was Cherokee for something probably not too nice, and said there must have been an Indian in the preacher's woodpile.

Of the two girls there wasn't no comparison as persons. Marge was worth a couple dozen Rose Jewels, with change due. But the only thing everyone commented on seeing them side by side was their looks.

"Why, they don't look like twins!"

"Why, ain't the light-haired one sweet!"

"Ain't Rose Jewel got the prettiest eyes!"

One Sunday after church let out and the congregation was all in the yard idling around, I said so everyone could hear, "Well, Rose Jewel may be the prettiest, but Marge's got the prettiest hair."

Rose Jewel bust out crying and went off behind the church to pout. Marge followed after her and told her that it wasn't true and I was just a kid and didn't know what I was talking about. She brought her back out to the yard and tried to get me to tell Rose Jewel that I didn't mean it. But I said, "I do so mean it, and furthermore Rose Jewel's fast!"

Well, Rose Jewel up and slapped me and stormed off. Marge didn't say nothing because she knowed it was the truth. But Monroe, he come over and pulled me aside and give me a hiding that near killed me. Probably would have if Mama hadn't stepped in between us and took up for me. She didn't blame me for saying it because she was the one said it first.

Mama didn't like any of the Starr family, and didn't trust any of the Pentecostal Holiness people, but only come to their church because the Baptist church was so far off. Brother Starr had tried to come courting her once, he a widower who took a deal of pride in his stock as a lady's man. Mama tried to put him off politely, but he persevered until she lost her patience.

"I'd as soon sleep with a toad," she told him finally, and that routed him.

Brother Starr had another daughter a couple of years older than the twins, Violet Ruby, the first of the preacher's flower and gemstone girls, and Monroe was kindly stuck on her too. But nobody knowed much about Violet Ruby because she was standoffish and booky. She was hailed far and wide as the greatest beauty of the county, and there wasn't a blemish on her skin, nor a part of her face nor body that was not perfect. Mama said Violet Ruby Starr was as cold as her name and the man who married her would freeze to the bedsheets.

It was true that in spite of her beauty few of the men dared brave her. One day when I was splitting kindling for the preacher, I overheard Violet Ruby say to Marge, "You show me the man I marry, and I show you the man I kill."

Marge answered her kindly sweetly, as was her nature. She said, "I like that Monroe. He's gentle and good."

Then Rose Jewel put in her two cents and said, "But I'm the one who'll get him."

And I said to myself, "Not if I have anything to do with it."

Marge was the only one of the Starr girls worth anything, but Monroe, he was tossed on the winds of love and doubt. Times he'd dream about Violet Ruby, the unattainable perfection; times he'd wallow in the splendor of Rose Jewel; and times he'd sit a fence rail with Marge, and the two of them would share just the most grandiose plans.

"I'm going to get me a ranch," he'd say to her, "with a couple of oil wells on it, or maybe more, and when they bring me in a gusher, I'll drill me another one."

Marge'd say, "I heard about this woman, Amelia Earhart, and she says that one day she's going to fly around the world. I'm going to do it, too."

Of course, none of it happened. Nothing ever does. But you got to dream. If you don't, why breathe?

Well, Brother Starr up and took his daughters and left Atoka. He had soured on the community and the Holiness Church because they didn't yell enough when they prayed and their testimonials begun to lack flair. He decided to go off to Los Angeles, California, where Sister Aimee Semple McPherson was recruiting sinners by the thousands to her Four Square Gospel Church. Times was growing harder in Oklahoma, and we was all of us feeling the pinch more each day. The rumors of California, of sun and rain and crops and sinners galore, presented a temptation that the preacher could not withstand.

Marge looked me up the day they was leaving and kissed me good-bye. She knowed the way I felt about her, and I guess she felt something for me too because she give me a new, blue bandanna wrapped with just the loveliest blue ribbon, and said, "Blue, I'll never forget you."

"You're damn right," I said, not knowing what else to say.

She said, "When we get settled, I'll write to you. Will

you tell Monroe where I . . . where we went? And here, give him this." She handed me a red bandanna tied with a red ribbon.

I said, "I wish you'd stay. If you did, you could marry Monroe and be my sister."

She said, "Well, he ain't asked me."

I said, "I'm asking you for him."

She said, "Blue, that ain't good enough. Besides, I don't love Monroe. And he loves Rose Jewel. Wouldn't you like Rose Jewel for a sister?"

I seen there wasn't no sense in talking to a brain that muddled with love and unselfishness, so I said good-bye. Then I wrote Monroe. He was in Tulsa trying to get work as a roustabout in the oil fields. I wrote, "You got to come home. Marge is gone." It was about as many words as I knowed how to spell.

Monroe was home within the week, dressed in black, thinking he was late to her funeral.

I said to him, "She ain't dead; she's gone!"

He hugged me to him in joy, then cuffed me a good one, saying, "Gone? Is that all she is? Where to?"

"Lost And Jealous," I said. Like I told you, I never did get that geography.

"Where's Rose Jewel?" Monroe asked. "Where's Violet Ruby? Where's the damn preacher?"

"They're all gone together."

"Who let them go?" he cried. Oh, he was fit to be tied.

He made inquiries around Atoka to folks more reliable than me and found out that they was indeed gone, and indeed bent on Los Angeles. But first, he found out, Brother Starr was stopping to visit his mother in a little

28

town called Tascosa, Texas, near Amarillo, to try to convince her to come with him. It seemed he thought his mother was something of a sinner herself and wouldn't be the worse for the trip.

"Besides," Mama said, "the old gal's probably got some money."

Monroe outfitted hisself for the trip to Amarillo, kissed Mama hello and good-bye, and hightailed it to the tracks of old Katy. I was right behind. You see, Monroe was a hero to me. Yet here he was always gone, always traveling away from me looking for work. This time maybe it was forever. Well, this time I was going with him. And that's how I happened to hop that freight that day.

There was no joy staying in Atoka. I would miss Mama, but now I knowed she would be well taken care of by Abe Boone. And I'd have paid hard cash to get away from them Boone boys. Abe may have been a good man, but I never seen such mean kids as them sons of his. Why, one time right after the wedding, Reg and Roy and Ray ganged up on me down to Boggy Crick and like to drown me with dunking before I grabbed me a willow branch floating by and whipped them till they squealed. Then when we got home, they made up this story about the welts I give them, making me out the villain. In spite of all I could say in my defense, Mama took up for them just to pacify Abe, and she give me a whipping which made me stand up for a week at the dinner table.

Truth to tell, Mama never did much favor me. Monroe was her boy. I took cuffings galore from her hand, but I never but once seen her lay even a finger on Monroe. That was the day we was all three sitting out on the front stoop, the hottest day, it seemed to me, in the history of mankind. Monroe took out a handkerchief and wiped his forehead and said, "Christ, it's hot!" Mama swung her arm around like a semaphore and just laid Monroe flat out.

"Don't you never let me hear you use His name in vain again, not the Savior's nor the Lord's neither."

I never seen her madder, but she was full of regret the very next second, seeing the split lip she had give her darling son. All that next week she couldn't do too much honeying Monroe. But I tell you, it stuck with me. Only once after that did I invoke the name of God. And then, I still pray, it wasn't in vain.

So shoot, with Mama so hard on me, and them devil Boone boys, there wasn't nothing anymore to tie me to Atoka. Though I have to say now that I soon enough did get homesick. That rubber factory in McAlester was a grim place, and when I looked in them cardboard cubicles and seen them dark people up against that brick wall, sitting staring at nothing, I was awful tempted to run back to Mama. It was just killing to the soul to see them.

It seems Bosco Pete was looking for someone in the rubber factory, ducking his head in first one then the next hole. But he didn't seem to rouse the party because we walked clear on through and out the back door without speaking a word to anyone.

We went back out to the Rock Island tracks, and me and Monroe followed him for a stretch until he took off on a trail leading down off the roadway into a grove of live oak and hickory. I could see a fire and lights of candles flickering down among the trees like fireflies and will-o'-the-wisps, and I stopped, thinking better of the whole thing. Why, Bosco Pete was nothing but a stranger to us, and where was he leading us to? Mama always told me, "You see a stranger, you give him a wide berth."

"Monroe!" I whispered, but Monroe was already following on down the trail. His back bled into the darkness, and then he was gone and the darkness closed in on me. Well, it was awful clammy, I tell you, and the wind was rising and fairly whistling along them tracks. I sure wasn't going to bed down up there alone. So I plunged down the trail after them and near run over Monroe, who was coming back to see what had become of me.

"Where you been?" he said. "If you ain't a nuisance!"

"I had to take a leak," I lied.

"Well, do it on your own time. Now come on. I smell mulligan."

We passed through the trees into a clearing, and this is where the candles was lit. There was about a dozen men lounging about a fire, sitting on rocks or boards or old tires or whatever there was to keep them off the ground, and all of them had a tin can or pie pan in their hands, eating out of it with a spoon. Bosco Pete either knowed a lot of these men before or he was fast introducing hisself, because everyone was welcoming him and calling him Pete right off, and he was already dishing hisself something out of the big pot by the fire.

"This here's Monroe M. Monroe," Bosco Pete said as we come into the firelight, "and that there's his kid brother Blue."

The men said, "Howdy, boys," and Monroe said howdy back, but I couldn't quite get up a voice yet.

A beefy, peg-legged man whose left leg was missing from

31

below the knee and left arm lopped off at the elbow, introduced hisself as Chicago Stumps and said, "You boys get yourself a plate there and get to busy and help yourself." He gestured to a tree that had a variety of "plates" hanging from it on nails. They was nothing but tin whatnots, but they served.

Monroe got him down a plate and one for me, and a couple of spoons that had seen better days, and cleaner, and he dished him up some of whatever it was in that pot. I hesitated, though, because in that black pot in the firelight it looked an awful lot like swampwater with chunks of rat and moss floating in it.

One of the men, who had hair that looked like it was brushed with axle grease, and teeth that looked so, too, he grinned and snorted, "Looks like the little one don't like our mulligan. Too good for it. You bring it over to me, sonny. I got just the place for it."

Stumps said to him, "Blade, leave him be." Then he said to me, "Go ahead, Blue, it's just good stew."

I spooned me up a little of it and could see when it got onto my plate that it was just that, good stew. And now I realized that I was awful hungry. I hadn't had anything to eat since breakfast, and that was just a biscuit sopped in gravy. I found me a rock on the edge of the circle of men and sat down to eat. The spoon and plate, I knowed, was not the cleanest and I remembered what Mama had always said, "Eat dirt, be dirt." But I was too hungry to mind.

As I ate, I listened to the men talk and watched them. They was a lively bunch, passing around a gallon jug of muscatel, with another couple gallons on the side waiting their turn. And my, wasn't they just full of the bulliest bull. They shared the news of the road, spicing it up more than a little, and told where there was work, and where there wasn't, and lots of other things besides, tales of disaster, mostly.

"Hey, Stumps," said one gangly, little, thin man they called Mile Away because of his smell. "Did you hear about Shorty?"

"Shorty who? Denver Shorty?"

"Baltimore Shorty."

"No, what happened?"

"Catching a manifest out of Spokane, he was so drunk he missed his grip, fell right into the wheels."

"No!"

"Yep. Lucky for him it was the last car and only the caboose rolled over him, cut his legs clean through at the thighs, just tendons holding them on. He dragged hisself off the tracks, his legs stringing along behind over the rocks and dirt, clear over to the brakey's shack, and that's where he finally passed out. The brakey took one look and he passed out, too."

"Shorty die?"

"No, they saved him. But he's sure got the right name now."

Mile Away laughed, and so did the rest of them, but none of them louder than Stumps. He slapped his knee with his one good hand, throwed his head back, and guffawed till the trees fairly shook and the leaves trembled. Me, I couldn't eat no more.

"Well," Stumps said, getting his breath back and going quiet and sad very quicklike. "You heard, I guess. Black Cully's gone."

The whole place quietened.

"No!" more than one said.

"No! Black Cully! No!"

"Coming over the Hump. Got hisself locked in a boxcar with nothing but a thin wool cardigan and a half gallon of Dago Red. It was thirty below on the Hump and he was froze solid when they opened up the car this side of the Rockies."

"Not Black Cully. He was a better hobo than that."

"It was a bull, had to be a bull."

"Damn, godforsaken bull."

"I'll tell you who it was, it was Rainbow Red, that's who it was."

"You're right, that's just who it was, Rainbow Red. That is the meanest bull west of the Rockies, and he wouldn't mind bashing your brains out and scrambling them for breakfast."

"Yes," said Stumps, "that's the talk, that it was Red. And you know yourself it was. Hell, Cully was planning on wintering in California. He wasn't planning no trip back over the Hump. It don't make sense. They say he was sleeping it off in a boxcar sidetracked in Rainbow when Red come across him, locked him in, and hitched up that car to the next manifest going east. Cully screamed all the way out of the yard, knowing where he was heading, but Red kept guard of that car and wouldn't let no one open it, just laughing as the train pulled out. It was murder, the coldest-blooded kind, and the rails all knowed it and let it happen."

Nobody said a thing more. They sat staring into the fire. The hair on my head was standing straight up, I tell you.

I had heard some talk about these bulls, or dicks as they was also called, detectives hired by the railroad companies to keep the hoboes off the freights. I knowed it was a mean, nasty, traitorous job, especially in these times when so many was having to hit the road. But the railroads wasn't having it easy either. They was going broke right and left because people wasn't traveling like they used to, leastways not paying people. And when the railroads closed down, more people was out of work, more people out looking for jobs. I understood why the railroad companies had to hire these detectives.

But I had never imagined a man like this Rainbow Red. I wondered if I would meet him ever. I prayed God I wouldn't.

Now, during all this talk I had been noticing some strange behavior in the camp, or the jungle as hobo camps along the railroads is called. There was this kid there, two, maybe three years older than me, tall and slight. I took him for the son of a man named Whitey because the two of them sat together, with Whitey's arm draped over the boy's shoulders the way a father will do his son. That is if a boy has a father, which I never did — or had too many fathers, perhaps I should say. In any case, Whitey and this boy was close.

And you remember this Blade fellow with the black

teeth I mentioned earlier. Well, he was sitting near Whitey and the boy, and I could see that he was watching them, slylike. Whenever Whitey turned away, following the conversation of first one man then the next, Blade would reach over and give this kid a playful sort of pinch and a gappy smile. The kid looked at him funny and pulled away, but he didn't say nothing to Whitey, and Whitey didn't seem to notice. Finally the kid got so aggravated by Blade's attentions that he stood up and skittered around the circle to another man they called Idaho Ed.

At this, some of the men done some throat-clearing and a few glances was exchanged. But no one said nothing and the conversation went right on, with Ed gathering the boy in his arms and the boy nestling in, glaring across the circle at Blade. Idaho Ed and Whitey looked at each other, and Whitey nodded, but he kept right up with the talk, throwing in a laugh or a question or a story of his own. I figured then that Idaho Ed was uncle to the boy.

I heard Blade say low to a man near him, "Looks like the gunsel is jumpy."

The man didn't answer but looked away. Whitey throwed Blade a look, but he didn't say nothing, only turned back to the talk. Then I begun to understand. I had heard tell of this kind of thing among men, and generally folks give it an ugly name and dropped their voices when they said it. I looked back to the boy in Idaho Ed's arms and then back to Whitey. They just seemed like people to me.

Now about this time come the end of the story about

Black Cully and Rainbow Red, and all the men sat shaking their heads, watching the fire flare and dwindle.

Blade said suddenly, "So Black Cully's dead! One less nigger."

If the jungle was quietlike before, now it was like a graveyard. Nobody moved. Finally Stumps said, without even looking at him:

"Blade, shut up."

"What'd I say?" Blade said. "Did I say anything wrong? I never meant to offend. Did I say anything to offend anyone in this august assembly?"

"Blade," Stumps went on, "it's true Cully was a nigger, but he was a good man. He had God's power in the warmth of his hands, and I wager there's hardly a man in this jungle didn't get healing from those hands at one time or another. We feel his loss very deep, and we don't want his name diminished in our company. I think I speak for every man here."

"You do," said the men. "You do."

"Well, I am sorry," Blade said, making it sound just so sincere and no more. "I didn't know this nigger had so many friends among my brethren of bums."

Now Whitey turned to him, and he spoke so hard and quiet and with such a fury that I forgot to breathe. "Now you see here, Blade," he said. "We won't sit here and be defiled by you. You are not our brethren, and we are not bums. We call ourselves hoboes. You come here and shared our food, and we give it gladly. You shared our fire and our company. And in return you give us your trash. Now you git!"

When he said this, Blade leapt to his feet and put his hand to his belt where his shiv hung. Whitey leapt up with him and faced him squared away.

"No man talks to me like that!" Blade said, spitting through his teeth.

"No man hardly talks to you at all," Stumps said, standing too. And so did the rest of the men all stand. "You been throwed out of every jungle in thirty states. Oh, get your hands off your belt, Blade! We know where you get your monicker, but we know too just how you use that blade. Stab men in the back, and then only when they're drunk."

"Git!" Whitey said again. "You been fouling our air too long."

Blade held a second, looking from man to man, then he grinned something awful and backed out of the group, snatching up a gallon of muscatel as he went. And still grinning, he backed out of the firelight into the blackness of the night.

Well! Watching him disappear all spooky like that, I sat there and shivered, and it wasn't from the cold. The men all looked each to the other, shifting around ill at ease the way chickens in a pen will do after a hawk flies over. Then one by one they sat back down and found a place to be comfortable. Chicago Stumps took up his place of prominence nearest the fire. The gunsel come back to Whitey, and the two resumed their cuddling. Idaho Ed didn't seem put out, so I guessed they had a good working arrangement among the three of them.

Little conversations started up here and there until finally the group regained its cheer. Presently Chicago

Stumps turned to Monroe and said, "So, Monroe Monroe Monroe, where you boys heading?"

I said "Amberillo" and Monroe said "Atoka" both at the same time. The men all laughed, and Monroe, he give me a sour look and then said, "Well, I'm going to Amarillo, but first I got to haul the brat back to Atoka."

"Too bad," Stumps said. "There's a manifest bound for Amarillo going through in about a hour. Could've took that."

"A manifest!" Monroe said.

I said, "What's a manifest?"

"You'd be in Amarillo tomorrow," Stumps said.

"Tomorrow!" Monroe said.

I said again, "What's a manifest?"

"You in a hurry, Monroe Monroe Monroe? By your name it don't sound like it." The men all laughed.

"Well," Monroe said, "there's this girl." The men all laughed again, and Monroe turned red. Even in the firelight I could see it. "Well, it's a couple girls, actual," he said. They laughed again.

"There's three of them, actual," I said, "but two of them's no good. He's going to marry Marge."

"You hesh!" Monroe said, then turned back to Stumps. "They're heading for California, but they're stopping first near Amarillo. I figure to catch them there because I may never locate them in California. I hear Los Angeles is mighty big."

"Oh, yeah!" A couple different men spoke up.

"That's why that manifest tonight is awful tempting."

"What's a manifest?" I said again, getting pretty mad. It was the gunsel, Whitey's boy, who finally answered me, the rest of them all continuing to talk across our heads. He said it low, but the sound of it come clear across the jungle to me because it was so different from the voices of the men, kindly soft, kindly clear.

"It's a train that don't stop," the gunsel said.

I looked at him with a curiosity, and that's the same way he looked back at me.

"A train that don't stop?" I said to him. "That don't seem likely."

"I mean it don't stop but once. At the end of the line. The next division."

"And that's Amberillo?"

"Yeah."

I said, "So it's a fast train, a manifest is?"

"Oh, yeah," the gunsel said. "Fastest way to get somewhere. If you're going somewhere."

Meanwhile, Monroe'd been talking with Stumps about it, and I heard him say, "No, it's too dangerous. He's only ten."

"I'm eleven!" I said.

"I don't care if you're ninety-nine, you're a kid and a pain, and I'm taking you back to Atoka."

"And miss the manifest!" I said. "Are you crazy? Do you want to lose them girls?"

"I told you hesh!"

"I'm taking a leak!" I said and got up and walked away with a man's dignity to do a man's job. I was kindly sly-like, figuring I'd give Monroe some time, let the boes do the talking for me. I remembered Earl's last words to me before I jumped off the train coming into McAlester: "You keep after him, kid. You do just fine." These was traveling men, and they liked traveling men. Give them five minutes with Monroe, and they'd talk sense into him.

Every time I stopped and looked back, that fire seemed so bright that I felt sure Monroe could still see me, so I drifted further and further away from the jungle. But turning the other way, the darkness was so deep that I felt it would just smother me. The moon had already gone down, and the stars was muted by a high haze. The air was thick and tasty, and smoke from the fire bent right down and rolled along the ground out to where I walked, coiling about my feet. It meant rain tonight. Away off to the southwest, some little lightning forks played.

Somewhere yonder an owl called with that soft *who, who, who,* that can send such shivers under your skin. Mama said they was the voices of murdered folk climbing out of their graves to seek their murderers. I thought about Blade and the knife hanging on his belt. He was a murderer, I was sure.

And then, just as though thinking about him had conjured him, there he was. I was almost in his arms before I knowed he was there, and then it was only by his stink. I couldn't see him because he was on the black side, but he had probably been watching me come toward him, backlit as I was by the fire.

"Well, hello!" he said, grabbing my arms tight up near the shoulders and breathing a truly poisonous wino breath into my face. "You comin' to see me?"

I didn't even think but sank to my knees as he closed in on me, planted myself firm into the ground, then pushed off with all my might and rammed my shoulder into the crotch of his pants so hard he lifted off the ground and flew backwards, squalling like a rabbit when you give it the chop. And I, meanwhile, hightailed it back to the jungle.

All the men was on their feet when I come running in, having heard Blade's squall. I was kind of prancing, I remember, the way a boxer dances around the ring after a knockdown, waiting to see if his opponent is going to get up again. I kept looking out to the dark.

"What happened?" Monroe said to me.

"It was an owl," I said. I was thinking fast here for a couple of reasons. Firstly, I didn't want these good fellows running out there after Blade like a bunch of vigilantes, getting theirselves cut up on his knife and killing him, which is what I knowed they was aching to do, every man of them. And mostly, I didn't want to ruin my chances of getting Monroe on that manifest. If he seen me getting in trouble every time I went off to take a leak, all the talking of all the boes on my behalf wasn't going to take.

"That was no owl!" Monroe said.

"I mean it was a rabbit," I said. "It was an owl and a rabbit. I seen the whole thing. This old hoot owl come swooping down on this rabbit, and it did screech so! Well, it was just a majestic kill. I just wish you all could've seen it, so I come running back to tell you."

They all stood staring at me, and Monroe, he looked at me sharplike, and truth to tell, I knowed I was overdoing it some.

"Blue," Monroe said, "are you telling a story?"

"What's that?" I said, pricking up my ears. Away off in the distance there was a train whistle.

"It's the manifest," Stumps said. "If you're going on it,

42

Monroe, you'd best hurry. It's going to pass here soon, and fast."

Monroe turned to that whistle, looking hungry. "No," he began, but his throat catched on something as he said it. "No, I guess I got a responsibility for Blue. I guess I'll trust the Lord to keep those girls in Amarillo until I can get there."

I said, "You *are* crazy!" Then I pulled him to one side and whispered to him sharp, "How long do you suppose I'm going to stay behind in Atoka now I've come this far? I'll be on that next train right after you. You going to leave me to ride these rails on my own?"

Monroe was on the verge now, and if I do say so myself who says it, I was making good sense. But I pushed it one final notch, nodding over to Whitey's boy, and lowering my voice even more.

"I guess I can make out though. A new gunsel's always welcome in the jungle, I guess."

Monroe reared back and give me a look near froze me, but I give him a big smile and said, "You want to know what almost happened to me just now, out there? And you want to know what I did? Let's us catch that manifest, and I'll tell you."

The train whistled again. Oh, it's such a sound, I can't tell you. The way it makes you go all cold and hot. It's the sound of plucking heartstrings.

Monroe said suddenly, "Whobody here can carry a message to Atoka tomorrow?"

Every hand went up. Shoot, they wasn't going nowhere anyways, and there was no better way to get a free meal than to carry a looked-for message. And I guess Mama

43

never brought a person inside her home she didn't feed. But for all that, these was good men, these boes, and they was glad to help.

Monroe grabbed Whitey and said, "Find Mrs. Lula Boone. Tell her Monroe's got Blue and we're safe, and tell her . . . tell her . . ."

I said, "Tell her we're gone west!"

Monroe said, ". . . and tell her to take care, and tell her we love her. You say it too, Blue."

I said, "Yeah, okay, tell her that. Come on, Monroe! We're going to miss that train!"

Four

THE HEAD OF THE TRAIN was just passing when we got up to the roadbed. The whole of the jungle emptied out to see us off, each just as excited for us as me and Monroe was for ourselves, each full of advice how to catch this manifest.

"Get yourself a gondola, but make sure —"

"No, a gondola's too open-air. Get yourself an empty reefer, and —"

"And get yourself killed? No, what you want is an oil tanker. It's a nice, smooth ride, and you get a little protection from the weather if you sit on the leeward walkway, and —"

"No, a gondola is your best bet, boys, and here comes a string of them, but make sure —"

But I didn't hear the rest. My mind was just a-whirl with it all, and here come the train, traveling fast. My breath was took away, watching her barrel down on us.

You see, a manifest is not like your regular freight train which is pulling out slow from the yard. She's a through train and just splendid the way she blazes through town.

45

Oh, she slows down some all right, but she steams up again just as soon as her nose smells countryside ahead because she's on a tight schedule, you see, and that engineer's anxious to get on home. Another thing, a local train like we rode north on Katy out of Atoka is hauling a lot of empty boxcars with their doors wide open and invitational, but a manifest is transporting commodities of one kind or another. She don't embarrass herself with empties to commode us boes. So all the weather that there is on those tracks, we gets.

The engine passes us by and I can see the engineer and fireman whip their heads around to look at us, like, "What's this? A parade?" And then they're gone and the string of gondolas heave up after. These is open-topped cars, and pretty easy to board, as a rule. But Monroe doesn't go for them. I looks at him and sees him glancing appraisingly back at me, and I sees at once what the trouble is here. He's beginning to think too hard again.

But now the gondolas is past and a string of closed boxcars follows, and I can tell from the clack of the wheels that she's picking up speed. Still I waits for Monroe. Still he hesitates. And all the men hollering, "Now! Now! Now!"

So I guess it's up to me, and finally when I sees another gondola bearing down, I gives a whoop and starts running. I hears Monroe yell, "Blue!" and then I hears the ballast crunching behind me, and I knows he's running too. I looks back to get a gauge on the front of the gondola, and she comes up next to me and I grabs on and gives a leap, and I'm up. I scrambles quick up that ladder to give Monroe room to get on, and he does, heaving up to the rung under me.

Why, it's ever so easy this time. I guess that's what comes of practice.

We whoops and hollers back to the boes of McAlester, but they're already swallowed up in the night, and we're on our own on those tracks.

I don't remember. I guess we laughed. I looked down at Monroe and he looked up at me, and I guess we laughed. I remember the wind. I could scarce breathe there for a second, trying to get my wind back after the run and the pure adventure of it. I throwed my head back, gasping. I can remember seeing the stars above, with embers from the engine mixed in, spewed high in the sky, twinkling on and off like they was all laughing with us. I can remember the sound of the train, just deafening. And I remember Monroe yelling.

"Get in, doggone you, Blue! I'm not going to hang out here all night."

I looked into the gondola. It was awful black down there. I couldn't make out what was inside, if anything, or how far down it was. Monroe give my butt a shove, and I bellied myself over the wall and dropped down into the gondola, landing on a load of something hard and tubular. Monroe come over now too, and he lit a match, and we seen that we was on a pile of four-inch cast iron pipes, each about ten foot long.

Well, now I know we did laugh. Our first bed out, and it's sewer pipes. But we settled down and was content. It may have been a hard mattress for a kid used to straw and ticking, but down below the walls of the gondola we did get some protection from the wind, and we was tired enough that soon the cast iron didn't seem so hard. We talked a bit, and Monroe, he scolded me for making the jump first before he was ready, and he told me I was a pest. But I couldn't have been happier, and I knowed he didn't really mean it.

I jumped up and went to the side of the gondola — the top of it come up to just above midthigh with me standing on the load of pipes — and I unbuttoned my fly and let go a whiz. Well sir, it's hard to describe the thrill of whizzing off a gondola flying sixty mile an hour, writing your name over a quarter mile or so of land. You'll just have to try it yourself someday.

I settled back down next to Monroe and he said, "Blue, that's the third time tonight. Your kidneys dribbling?"

I laughed and explained that I hadn't yet gone. Then I told him about being out in the dark with Blade, and what happened between us. He listened careful and didn't interrupt. When I come to the part where I rammed Blade in the crotch, Monroe said, "Who taught you that trick?"

I said, "I don't know. I guess I made it up on the spot."

He said, "Good job."

I laid back on the pipes, propping my head up against the end wall of the gondola. The stars and embers kept flying by, though now the stars was beginning to be hid more and more by gathering clouds. And every once in a while there'd come a flash of far-off lightning, and it was just a fine, fine show.

Little by little by these lightning flashes I come to have a pretty good idea what our gondola looked like. It was the same length and width of a regular boxcar, sixty foot by eight. We was at the forward end, and my, didn't it look long in the lightning. The piles of pipes, lashed together in bundles to keep them from shifting, stretched length upon length down the car, making it appear even longer. I've seen paintings by those fellows, what they call those surrealist fellows, that draw everything out longer and thinner and pointier than they really are, and that's what those cast iron pipes in that rusty old gondola looked like.

But you know, it's wearying to a kid that age, being in so much gloriousness, and by and by, in spite of all I could do to stop it, my eyelids started feeling awful weighty. And I dropped off, dead to it all.

And dead I almost was, too. I don't know how much time went by, but I come awake to the most godawful, heart-stopping clamor you ever heard. It was a rumble at first, and I guess that's what woke me. Then some crashes and a hard, heavy rattling. That's when Monroe woke.

"What's that?" he said.

And then come a flash of lightning, brighter than the rest, and we seen what it was. Down at the other end of the gondola, the pipes was loose and rolling, just writhing, it looked like in the lightning, like a bed of black snakes. The lashing on that end pile must have broke.

Then the lightning was gone and we was left again with just only the blackness and the rumbling and crashing as the pipes settled and rolled and smashed up against the steel sides of the gondola. And then the train lurched and I heard a clatter and a *whoosh*, and slam! One of the pipes shot the length of that gondola like a rocket, striking the wall beside my head with a blow that rattled my teeth. A foot more my way and my face would have been printed on the wall.

The pipe ricocheted back and swiped my left shin as it went and I thought I was crippled. I bawled out with pain and grabbed my leg.

Monroe said, "Where is it?"

"My leg."

"Can you walk?"

He helped me up, and I found that I could move it all right. Nothing seemed broke. But I could feel a wetness in my shoe. I guessed it was blood, though there was always the possibility it was that other thing.

"We got to get out of here fast," he said, pushing me to the wall where the ladder was. "Any second one of them pipes —"

And just then one of them pipes did. In a flash of lightning so long and forked that it lit us up like day, the train took a dip and a pipe come caroming down the length of that car ripping out every lashing in its path. The bundles broke and the pipes started rolling every whichaway. The gondola was awash with them, making such a din you'd have thought heaven had met hell. The pipes under us give way as they lost their saddles, and but for our being at the ladder and grabbing hold of the top of the wall, we'd have been drug under and rolled out like pie crust.

Monroe shoved me over first, and I clambered out of that gondola the way a spider leaves a flushed toilet. Monroe was right after me. We clung onto the ladder, breathing hard and listening to the rhubarb on the other side of that steel wall. My, it was fierce. It's a pure wonder that those gondolas are reusable. Sewer pipes, too.

Then come a bolt of lightning so straight down and electric it near blinded me, followed hard on by a clap of thunder so mighty it like to bust my eardrum, which was already near split by the kettledrum I was riding. And the sky opened up and poured.

Now you never seen rain until you seen rain in Oklahoma. It comes down in sheets and buckets, just slinging cats and dogs at you. It's a blessing people survive it. Clinging onto the ladder outside that gondola, I couldn't have wished for a worse time for it.

Monroe yelled to me, "Rain!"

I yelled back, "I know!"

He yelled, "I don't know where to go!"

I yelled, "Somewhere else!"

There was only one way to start, and that was forward, jumping the coupling gap to the next car. This would have been hard for me without Monroe because I just didn't have the length for it in the arms and legs. But once Monroe made the jump, he lent me a hand. We climbed the ladder to the top of the car and crawled onto the catwalk, and there we perched, rocking on the top of that locomoting train like the cradle just before it fell.

The lightning now was coming so fast and thick that there was scarce any darkness at all anymore. The top of the train stretched out before and behind in that orange glare, like we was on our way to hell. And we was right in the thick of it, too, with the thunder not waiting at all but sounding right on the heels of the lightning. Up there on that catwalk, nothing around us but storm, I thought the next bolt would strike me clean, slap down through my punkin head.

I yelled, "We can't stay here!"

Monroe yelled, "We can't go nowhere!"

I looked at the gondola of sewer pipes behind us, and it was just rolling. Monroe yelled, "I left my packsack in there! I had ten dollars in it!"

I yelled, "You going back for it?"

He yelled, "You think I'm crazy?"

And so he turned and we started crawling forward. Somewhere up there ahead, a lot of boxcars away, was that string of gondolas that passed us back in McAlester. With maybe a miracle, one of them might be empty or loaded with something soft. Anything but sewer pipes.

The catwalk was slippery with rain, so I gripped on tight. We was wet through, and the cold and wind was severe, and we begun shivering with it. I gripped the cat-walk tighter still. When we come to the end of the boxcar, Monroe jumped first and then me, him ready to catch me on the next catwalk. It was slow work, and dangerous, but car after car, we made our way forward.

I don't know how long we crawled or how many cars we put behind us, but it seemed at least a night's worth. The storm began lessening as we went, the train steaming through the eye of it and leaving the worst behind. The lightning come less often and the wait for the thunder growed longer, and the rain thinned out some. Back in the east behind us, it was beginning to grow light. And still we crawled.

Then, in the dimness of dawn, we seen something up ahead on the catwalk, something dark and hunkered over.

When we got nearer, the lightning flashed again and it reared up and looked at us and give us a gappy grin. It was Blade.

"Well, if it ain't the boys!" he says, and breaks into a squeal of a laugh.

Me and Monroe stops dead. Monroe says kind of careful, "Hello, there. Glad to see you."

"Glad to see me?" Blade says, and laughs again. I sees he's got his gallon of muscatel with him still, though it's near gone. I figures that's either good for us, or very bad.

"We was beginning to feel kindly lonesome up here," Monroe says, attempting a laugh.

"Oh, it's lonesome, all right," Blade says. "Nobody here but us." Then he looks to me and says, "Why, you brought your gunsel with you. Good, nothing like a nice, warm little body to fire you up on a cold night like this."

Monroe stiffens, but he don't say nothing. Blade says to me, "You know, you wasn't very nice to me back in Mc-Alester. If you brung them boes down on me, you know what they'd have done?" He grins again.

Monroe says, "We don't want no trouble, Blade! We just want to ride!"

"What kind of trouble did you have in mind, sonny?" Blade grins, and he reaches slow under his coat.

Well, I'm no fool. From the first I knows what he's been leading to, and I'm set for him. I already gots my Barlow slipped out of my pocket with the long blade folded out. So now when Blade draws out his shiv, I says, "Monroe!" and I slaps the handle of the Barlow into his hand.

Monroe crouches to spring, and so do I. He's got one hand gripping a slat of the catwalk, and the other with the Barlow stuck straight out in front of him at Blade's face. When Blade sees it, his grin closes up and his eyes get hard.

"Oh," he says, slowlike, "I see you got an equalizer!" Then he grins again. "Think you're man enough to use it?"

I says, "Try him!" Monroe gives a little wave with the Barlow. Blade watches Monroe's eyes a long minute, then he relaxes a little, backing down.

"Well, you boys sure is quick to take offense!" he says, and gives another squealy laugh.

Monroe says, "Back up, Blue. We'll ride another car."

Still crouching, I starts backing up, and so does Monroe. But Blade, he keeps grinning and squealing and he scoots along the catwalk after us, still with his shiv in his hand. We come to the end of the car, and it seems we're cornered.

"Jump!" Monroe says to me, but I hate to do it because it leaves him alone on the car with Blade, and he has to turn his back on him to make his jump.

I whispers in his ear, "You jump right after. I'll catch you when you land."

I makes the jump, then turns quick, and Monroe he comes right after, springing backwards off the catwalk, trusting I'll be there. He wobbles when he lands, but I catches onto his belt and holds him steady, and we're safe on the end of our car. Blade faces us from the end of his car, looking sour across the coupling gap into the point of the Barlow in Monroe's hand. And now it's our turn to laugh.

54

"Come ahead, Blade!" Monroe yells. "You just try it!"

Blade snarls. Then he grins again, that infernal, doggy grin. And he sits down flat on his catwalk. And he starts to wait.

Five

So HERE'S ME and Monroe facing off Blade on the top of that speeding train. As I told you, the day was coming on and the light was getting thicker by the minute. Little by little I could see the countryside around us define itself, life wakening up. We was on the outskirts of a town, and it seemed a sizable one, stretching off to the north. I judge now that it was Oklahoma City, but as we didn't stop, I didn't know at the time.

We was passing a few outlying houses, and people was getting up and starting their morning chores. We went whizzing by them and they looked up at us, the three of us crouched on our catwalks, knives aimed at each other's faces. But they couldn't do nothing for us but gape. We was on top of a moving train, and it was lawless up there.

Little by little we settled down, going gradual from a crouch to a sit. Monroe and Blade lowered their knives, keeping them at the ready on their knees. But none of us took our eyes off the other. Blade kept taking slugs of his muscatel until the bottle was empty. Then he tossed it into the coupling gap, and it shattered and was gone.

By and by my eyes begun to grow heavy again, though you might wonder how I could think of sleep. But I was only eleven and it had been the longest day and night I ever wanted to see, and my bones was so weary and cold they ached. I slipped from my sitting position to a kind of a left-sided curl, wrapping one arm around Monroe's waist to keep the train from bucking me off.

Blade grinned at me, and I sat right back up again and shook my head to clear it. That old devil. He was just waiting for us to fall asleep.

But I couldn't keep it up. I said, "Monroe, I'm just going to lay down here a minute and rest my eyes, but I won't be asleep." And I curled round him again.

Monroe said, "Take my belt and tie yourself to the catwalk. You'll go to sleep sure, and roll off."

"I'm not going to tie myself down here with him sitting over there like a turkey buzzard!"

"You do as I told you!"

So I slipped off his belt, which was just a hank of rope as I told you before, and I looped it around one of the slats in the catwalk and tied myself down, suspecting as I did so that it was pure suicide. But I was too sleepy to fuss. I laid down and looked over at Blade. He didn't look so good hisself. He snorted at me, then he laid down too, keeping his eye, which was bleared and rheumy with drink and the cold, level with mine across the gap. I swore to myself that I would not close my eyes, and I stretched them open wide and wished for a couple of toothpicks.

"Monroe," I said. "Talk."

"What do you want me to talk about?"

"I don't care. Tell me about Tulsa. Tell me about

Chicago Stumps. Tell me about hoboes. Tell me what that Whitey fellow meant, what he said to Blade about hoboes and bums."

Blade snorted again. "Whitey ain't a hobo. He's a punk."

Monroe said, "Shut up, Blade, me and Blue's talking." Then he said to me, "Well, Blue, I don't rightly know, but the way I understand it, there's a kind of pride among hoboes."

Blade snorted again.

"A hobo, you see," Monroe went on, giving Blade a flash of the Barlow, "is a kind of a migrant worker. He works a job out, then he goes. He goes cause he's seeking more work, and more work, and on down the line. You could call *us* a hobo, I guess, Blue. It's the times. But a hobo's different from a tramp, which is a kind of a migrant *non*worker, I guess you'd say, who's got his own kind of pride. He don't work; he just goes. And then a bum, he's a *non*migrant *non*worker. He don't work and he don't go neither."

Monroe probably said more, but I never heard it. These traitorous, lazy eyes must have closed on me because the next thing I knowed, it was later. Hours later, judging from the position of the sun high overhead. The train was still clipping along, and I was still tied to the catwalk, but I was alone.

I sat up and about swooned from it. I ain't never been so sore and achy. My shin was swoll from where the sewer pipe had struck it, and there was clotted blood all over my cuff and shoe.

I looked both ways, but there was no sign of Monroe or

Blade. Well, my eyes just flooded up with tears and I choked so I scarce could breathe, but sobbed instead. There wasn't a question in my mind about what had happened. Monroe had fell asleep too and Blade had jumped him, and the two together fighting had rolled into the coupling gap and then onto the tracks. And me sleeping through it all.

Sitting there blubbering, I looked up and seen this figure away off in the distance climbing the side of a boxcar and mounting the catwalk. It was Blade sure, or a bull, coming to get me.

I tried to untie the rope holding me to the catwalk, but it had got wet and the knot was swoll tight. The figure was getting closer, running along that catwalk at high speed. I felt for my Barlow but remembered I had give it to Monroe. I clawed at the knot with my fingernails, but it wouldn't loosen.

About then I heard my name called, and I looked up and looked again, and it was Monroe. Well, I started bawling all over again.

He come up and put his hand on my shoulder and said, "What's wrong with you?"

I said, "I thought you was dead."

He said, "Shoot!"

I took me a minute and got my breath back. He looked away and, oh, whistled or something. Then I said, "Where's Blade?"

He said, "Oh. Gone."

I said, "Gone where?"

He said, "Don't you worry. He won't bother you no more."

59

I didn't ask for details. I didn't want to know. But I hoped for Monroe's sake that Blade had just fell asleep and rolled off the catwalk. I didn't want a killing on his conscience.

Monroe said, "Come on. I found us a place to ride."

He untied the knot for me and freed me from the catwalk. I didn't ask him what happened to my Barlow. I just followed him forward, jumping car to car, until we come to that string of gondolas up front. They was full of coal. We hopped over and climbed into the back one, and it wasn't bad. Sure did beat strapping yourself to the top of a boxcar.

But there was all this coal dust blowing all over and getting into our eyes and mouths. I said, "Wouldn't it be less blowy in that head gondola?"

Monroe allowed that it would. And so we clambered over one gondola of coal after another until we reached the first one. By that time we was so black all over that we was indistinguishable from the coal itself, and even if a bull had come looking for us in that very car, he'd not have spied us.

We nested down among them lumps of coal, and though I can't speak for Monroe, I know I slept like one of them.

I woke just as we was pulling into Amarillo late in the afternoon. There's something about the change of speed on a train, the break of rhythm, that wakes you every time.

Now Amarillo lies just about in the center of the Texas Panhandle, and but for a griddle, there's nothing flatter nor hotter in this world. Early June is ordinarily tolerable in Oklahoma and Texas, but these was bad times in more than just money ways. This and the Oklahoma Panhandle to the north is the heartland of what they come to call later the Dust Bowl, a dry, windy, harsh country, and a sad place to call home.

But it wasn't always so. It had been good prairie land, tall and wavy with the natural prairie grasses, then good cattle land with fine grazing, then good wheat land, just rich with grain. But just as though the country's Depression had depressed nature, it stopping raining. The soil dried out. Or when it did rain, it was in torrents and the dry ground couldn't absorb the water, but run off with it in the flood. Then the freeze come and pulverized the soil. Then the sun come back and baked it to powder. Then the winds come and blowed it away. Why, they said a full half of Texas, all of its topsoil, blowed right out of the state. And in Kansas City they had to import Texas agents to sell the Texas real estate that had blowed into town.

When me and Monroe hit Amarillo, it was right in the thick of it. The drought had been on about three years and the people was feeling the pinch pretty severe — no water, no crops, and not much help from anywhere. Some of them relocated, selling or losing their lands to the feds, but among many there was still a feeling of optimism. "Next year . . ." they'd say. You could hear it all around you, "Next year . . ." And they come to be known as the Next Year People.

But to a little hick kid who hadn't never seen so much as a traffic light before, well, Amarillo was just a grand town. Tall buildings all around. Automobiles spinning by. Neon lights flashing even in the daytime.

We hit the ground before the train had stopped and was off to find our way to Tascosa, which, if you'll remember, is where Monroe had found out Preacher Starr's mother had her home. We looked for a jungle to clean up in, but we didn't find none. You see, hoboes generally make their jungles around water, some little crick or irrigation ditch, or what have you. But around Amarillo there ain't no water, or wasn't then at any rate, so Lord knows what the boes did but go dirty.

We stopped at a filling station to use their facilities, but we was run off by the owner. Now, on the whole folks was much kinder, much more generous in those days than what you ordinarily find today. They had to be. There was a sense of pulling through together. But I guess the sight of us two soots heading for the john was a mite upsetting to these good folk, cause we didn't even make the door.

"You git!" That was all we heard, because we got.

Treated so bad, we decided we'd go ahead and start walking to Tascosa and would soon find us a nice waterway, and there we would clean up and be beholding to no man nor filling station. But we walked and walked, and the houses thinned out, and the afternoon sun fried us, and there was no sign of a river, crick, nor mud puddle, and all in all I'd say that I had spent many a happier day. Monroe took up walking upwind, declaring that I was getting riper by the hour and unless I washed my pants soon, he was going to start calling me Mile Away, too.

I was about to perish of thirst. And my stomach begun thinking my head was disconnected, because it had been a worrisome long time since I had sent any food on down.

Finally I stopped and said, "Monroe, see that house over there? I am going to ask them for water. And if they don't give it to us, I am going to steal it."

He didn't try to stop me, but hung back as I went to the door. A woman come at my knock. She was a tall, lean, scraggle-haired woman who looked, as Mama would've said, like she'd been rode hard and hung out wet. Even through the screen of the door, I could see a brittleness in her eye, and I said to myself, "Huh-oh, Blue, you picked yourself a mean old gal here!"

She give me a long, sour look, a sort of horrified look, I thought, then said, "You get over to that pump, young man!"

I didn't pause, but did as she said. She slammed out the screen door after me and then seen Monroe and pulled up short.

"Who are you to him?" she said to Monroe.

"I'm his brother."

"You may be," she said, "but you certainly ain't his keeper! Just look at the two of you, black as niggers in a coal chute! Why, I'd be ashamed! Just what have you been doing? And just where . . ."

And on she rattled. All the time she talked I was manning her pitcher pump, drawing up bucketfuls of water which Monroe carried around back of the house to empty into a number three zinc washtub she set up next to the clothesline. There was a gourd dipper on the pump, too, and both of us took big drinks.

". . . I never seen the like, a growed boy like you . . ."

And she threw us a bar of Fels-Naptha and disappeared into the house, still talking. There was a trough for the cow nearby with standing water warmed by the sun, and we relocated some of it into our cold well water and took us the bath of our lives. I finished up and jumped out and was just reaching for my clothes, and Monroe was just standing up to get out of the water, when the woman come slamming back out the screen door, jabbering like a jay. Monroe sat with a splash back into the black water, and I covered myself as best I could with my hands.

"You're not thinking about putting them filthy clothes back on! Why, you ninnies! You smell like an outhouse!"

And she tossed some garments on the ground and slammed back into the house. It was a pair of overalls and a chambray shirt for me, and some khakis and a hickory shirt and B.V.D.'s for Monroe, out of her husband's drawer I guess. They wasn't sized just right, and they was anything but new, but they was clean.

When we was dressed, Monroe rolled up his dirty clothes into a pack to save for washing because they was good blue denims and in pretty good shape, though so dirty. But he made me take my trousers, which wasn't much but rags anyway, over to the outhouse and drop them down the hole. Now this outhouse wasn't the family's current commode but was an abandoned old two-seater, so Monroe and me took advantage of the convenience and relieved ourselves. And it was an awful welcome relief, too.

Then we went up and knocked on the door, and the woman come back out to us. She took her hand and screwed my head around and looked behind my ears, then said disappointedlike, "Well, I guess your Mama taught you something anyways."

Monroe said, "We want to thank you, ma'am, for your hospitality."

She said, "Humph! Here!" And she give him a pound coffee can with a bread wrapper over it. "I expect you're hungry."

"Well," Monroe said, and I don't believe I ever seen him so at a loss for words. "Thing is, you see, I lost my packsack on the train, and I don't have any . . ."

"Oh, I'm sure you did!" she said. "But what are we going to do about that?"

"What I mean is —"

"Oh, hesh!"

Monroe said, "Well, we thank you kindly."

And I said, "Thank you kindly."

"Where do you think you're going in them shoes?" she said, pointing to my feet. "I never seen such a pair of nothings."

I said, "Well, I'll guess they'll do for a while."

"Here," she said, and thrust a pair of shoes into my hand. They was just exactly the right size and, though they was high-button shoes and must have been near as old as me, they was hardly worn. I looked up at her, but seen her eyes shining something awful, and I looked away. She turned of a sudden back into the house, saying, "Good-bye, boys," and closed the door quick behind her, though I could hear her just inside backed up against it, crying. I felt like crying myself, having misjudged the woman so just because she wore a hard look.

I knelt and put on the shoes and buttoned them up, taking off the ragged pair Mama give me. They did feel good.

"Whose do you suppose they were?" I whispered to Monroe.

"I don't know," he whispered back.

"Do you think I should take them?"

"She give them to you, didn't she? Who do you suppose she wants to have them?"

As soon as we got a proper distance down the road and out of sight of the house, we stopped and sat on a rock by the roadside and ate the grub the woman had fixed us. It was nothing but a biscuit apiece sopped in bacon grease and a potato to share, but we hadn't ate nothing since that mulligan, so it tasted awful good.

I thought about that woman, whose name I never did learn, and I wondered, as I have wondered all these years since, what her sorrow was. But that was her story. My story went on down the road to Tascosa.

Back on that road, after downing the woman's food, we wasn't walking long before a car come along, a slick little '32 forked-8 Ford. A man by name of Abner something give us a ride all the way to Tascosa. He's the only man I ever seen could talk without ever stopping, getting up a voice breathing out or breathing in, just like a harmonica. It was just extraordinary watching him do it. He told us every speck of news about Tascosa, but he didn't seem to know a thing about Clyde Starr or his girls. Yes, he knowed Mrs. Edwina Starr, the preacher's mother, and could describe in detail every stick of furniture in her house, and went on to do it. But he had been out of town for several weeks, down below San Antone drumming Oxydol store to store for Procter & Gamble, and he didn't know the latest, but would be glad to stop in with us at

Mrs. Starr's to catch up, and was any of these Starr gals single?

Edwina Starr was a genteel old lady who lived in a little frame house which had most of its paint gone with the wind. I don't believe I ever come across a pokier talker anywhere on the continent, with a drawl that stretched clear to Georgia, adding on three or four extra syllables to every word, and a couple extra words to every phrase.

"Naoh, suh, maiy deauh suhon Cuhlyuhd hayas gaown aown tuhoo the stayate of Cayalifaowniuhuhuh."

Well, Monroe and I about died. "He's gone on to California?" Monroe said. "When?"

"Aoh, leuhssuhee, ah guheuhs uhit wuz yuheuhstuhduhauh."

"Yesterday? Did he say where he was going?"

"Laowsangeluhees suhomewheyuhuhuh."

"He didn't give you an address?"

"Nayow, lehussuhee. Huhee duhid muhenshuhen thayat pruheachuh wouhman, thayat Suhiuhstuhuh Aiuhmuhey."

"Aimee Semple McPherson?"

"Thayat's huhuhuh. And thayat's aowl ah knaoh."

It seems the preacher tried to get his mother to go along with him and the girls to be saved at the Four Square Gospel Church. But she said no, she had lived in Texas all her life, and she would die there, saved or not.

We left Edwina Starr's house feeling down and dreadful. Was we going to chase after them all the way to California, or was we going to give it up? And just how was we going to be able to find them in a town as big as Los Angeles?

Abner, of course, was in hog's heaven. He had got an earful of gossip and was primed for a week. We parted company on the road in front of Mrs. Starr's house, him wishing us luck in our pursuit and us wishing him luck with his Oxydol. We headed back for Amarillo, but I just have no idea where Abner went to.

Six

It was good and dark now, and there wasn't no chance of getting a ride back to Amarillo at this hour, so me and Monroe looked for a place to bed down. Well, there wasn't no lack of shelter in this part of the land because a lot of farms had been abandoned. Or not abandoned so much as that the owners had been drove off their land or tricked out of it by the federal government.

You see, these was political times, and the politics got pretty dirty about now. The fellow we had in the White House was Franklin Delano Roosevelt, and he was a pretty good man in lots of regards. I have no doubt but that he was doing what he thought best, and was pushing his relief programs through Congress as fast as he could. But to the little farmer, there was mighty little relief. The people who needed it most got it last and least, as a rule.

Mortgages fell due and these fellows in the Resettlement Administration just gobbled up the farms, giving precious little in the way of payment because they knowed the farmers was desperate and would take any little something rather than lose everything altogether. And then the farmers was shoved off their lands. Maybe they went west to California like the Starrs, or maybe they drifted into lost clusters like those folks in the rubber factory in Mc-Alester, or maybe all they knowed to do was put a bullet in their heads.

It was the Resettlement Administration's stated plan for soil conservation in the Dust Bowl to double the size of the farms. Well, any fool with half a brain for arithmetic knows that the only way to double the size of the farms is to halve the number of farmers. It's an awful cold and cruel policy, I say.

And then once the feds gained the property, a dozen acres here and a dozen acres there, a dozen acres everywhere but none of them connected, they just let them sit there in the weather. They didn't plant them, which would have helped hold the soil in the wind. They didn't use the Chiseler on them, which plowed up big clods to help hold what little rain they got and protect the young plants. No, they just let the dirt blow. So on the next farm where the farmer did plant and did chisel, he just sits when the wind comes and watches it pick up speed on those abandoned acres next door, and pick up dirt and drop it on his land, killing his crop. Then, with a killed crop, he's got nothing to hold his own soil anymore, and the next wind comes up and now he watches his own land blow away. Then the next year he loses his farm. And there's another empty building for Monroe and Blue to bed down in.

Of course I didn't know this then. All I knowed was that I was awful tired and awful glad to find this empty farmhouse. There was old straw in the barn and a roof overhead. Monroe and me curled up together for warmth and slept hard till morning.

In the morning's light we found last year's garden behind the house, and we gathered up some turnips and onion greens. I don't guess I've ever had truck any pithier or more bitter, but my stomach was so angry now that it couldn't complain any louder.

We hit the road back to Amarillo, and it was just a sparkling clear day, the morning air cool and fresh. Monroe, with a night's sleep behind him and food in his belly, had a lighter frame of mind and begun whistling "Red River Valley" double-time as we walked.

"Well, what do you say, Blue?" he said. "You want to string along with me to California?"

I said, "Well, I don't care if I do."

So I guess our minds was made up. And now I started whistling along with him, and he pulled his harmonica out of his rolled-up, coaly denims. He had to blow it out some to get rid of the coal dust, but it played okay, and ain't no one could blow a French harp better than Monroe. He took up the song, and although I have never been able to carry a tune more than halfway, I joined in singing, and my, that "Red River Valley" is about as gay a walking tune to such dismal sentiments as you may find anywhere.

> From this valley they say you are going,
> We will miss your bright eyes and sweet smile,
> For they say you are taking the sunshine,
> That has brightened our lives for a while.

Presently the road took a bend, and we hove into parallel with a pair of railroad tracks. "These," I said to myself, "is the very tracks which will carry us to California." And I sung even louder. Up ahead I seen the first tall buildings of Amarillo, standing up out of that flat countryside, and further on a range of black mountains.

"Say, Monroe," I said, "I don't remember them mountains up ahead. Ain't they pretty?"

Monroe, he was bound up in his song and didn't answer me but kept blowing. I joined back in.

> Come and sit by my side if you love me.
> Do not hasten to bid me adieu,
> But remember the Red River Valley
> And the boy who has loved you so true.

And now I looked again, and darned if those mountains didn't seem about twice't as high and twice't as close as they did before, like they was laying right the other side of town.

And here come an old '28 Whippet rattling right fast toward us, her bumper held on with baling wire, and her engine running only on a prayer. She stopped when she got to us, and I seen a good-looking young family inside, man and a woman and three little kids.

The man said, "Don't you boys see that duster coming? You better get in here and come along back with us to Tascosa. We got a shelter."

So we looked again, and we seen now that sure enough those wasn't mountains at all but clouds of dirt. They looked, oh, several hundred feet high, billowing up and just sailing in the wind, coming slap toward us. The woman was looking back with her eyes wide and rolling, kind of comical you know, and the three kids was sticking their heads out the windows and pointing back and laughing.

Monroe said, "Thank you, but we're going to California."

The man said, "You're a fool!"

The woman said, "Stanley, leave them be! We gots to go!"

He said to us, "You'd best come now!"

But Monroe said again, "Thank you, kindly, but we got business in California."

The man put his Whippet into gear, and the old car give a cough, apologetic the way all those old Whippets was, and they chugged off. Me and Monroe, we turned around and started walking again right in the face of that roller.

Now, I can't account for our stupidity in any way but to say that we was just fool kids. This was not our country and we didn't have no idea what it was coming at us. The morning had been so sunshiny and the air so fair that it just didn't seem possible to us that there could be a danger in the world.

But as the duster got nearer, we begun to rethink it. Now it come tumbling over Amarillo, and those grand, tall buildings looked like blades of grass in the path of a steamroller. The dust churned them under, obscuring them altogether. And now that we got a perspective on it, we could see that those billows was much higher than we thought before. Much higher. They must've been thousands upon thousands of feet tall, just filling the sky, and looking so dark and mean that we stopped, us two kids, and watched them loom up over us. The sun went down behind them, just as though it was a vast mountain range, and for a moment we was standing in a twilight.

And now the advance winds hits us. They's kindly pleasant for a moment, kindly warm, a swirly type of wind. But they gets stronger fast and starts picking up the lighter soil and debris, straw and stick, and flinging them up into our eyes. We turns our backs to the wind, and blinks, and rubs at our eyes to clean them out.

And while our backs is turned the real wind hits us, strong gusts that picks up not just the dust, but the sand and loam, so that the air gets simply filled with the land as the roller tumbles over us. In the time it takes to snap your fingers, all light is gone, and it goes black as midnight.

I turns around and reaches out to grab onto Monroe so as not to lose him, but he's gone, swallowed up in the dirt. I can't see him. I can't even see my hand there stretched out in front of me. I grabs out here, and turns and grabs out there, but I don't find him. I opens my mouth to call and it fills up with dirt, just that fast. I chokes, and turns my back again to the wind, and spits. I can't get a breath. It seems like the air is so full of dirt, there's no air left in it.

And such a howling of wind and hissing of sand, blasting my skin raw till the blood starts out of it. And such a heaviness, with all that dirt above weighting down on me.

I starts to panic. I can't breathe, I can't see, I can't hear nothing but the screaming wind, I'm hurting. If you ever seen a horse in a lightning storm, that's me. I bolts. I don't

74

know where I'm running to but I just gots to go. Maybe I think I can find Monroe. Maybe I think I can outrun the storm and get back out to that sunshiny, clear day I was just in the middle of. Maybe I don't think at all but just runs.

I runs into a ditch and takes an awful spill, skinning my knees and arms bad, banging my bones into the rocks. But I'm right up and running again. And now I runs straight into a barb wire fence, and it breaks and I falls through it. The strands spring up around about my head and slap at my face and eyes. I tries to roll away. But the barbs catch in my clothes and cut into my skin, and the wires coil around my legs and arms and neck. I fights to get loose, but I can't see nothing, and I gets tangled faster and faster. Finally I falls back into the dirt, wore out, and lays there heaving, trying to get air.

And laying there, finally my mind starts working again, and I come little by little back to my senses. I slips the bandanna Marge give me up over my mouth and nose, and presently I starts to breathe again, shallow little breaths that makes my chest ache with wanting more. Taking as much care of the barbs as I can, I curls up in a ball with my back to the wind, and ducks down my face and covers it over with my arms.

And here I waits.

Seven

It was a long wait. I don't suppose it could've been more than a couple of hours before the storm calmed enough to see at all, but laying there like the dead in it, feeling the dust and sand drift up heavy against my back burying me, it seemed like days and days. I had a lot of time to wonder at it. To wonder where on earth such a thing come from and where in hell it was going to. Some said these dusters was the wrath of God on our unholy planet, but I can't hold with that. I say God didn't have nothing to do with it, because if He's that mean and low-down, I don't want nothing to do with Him.

I wondered about Monroe, where he was, if I would ever see him again. I wondered about the good-looking young family in the old Whippet, if they made it to their shelter. I wondered about Edwina Starr, if the drawly old gal had got her windows shut in time against the storm. I wondered about Abner's slick little forked-8 Ford, if Abner had a garage for it or if it was sitting out on the street getting its paint sandblasted. I wondered about Mama, how she was, and if she was wondering about me.

Once, when the howling of the wind seemed less fierce, I raised my head and opened my eyes. The dust was still blowing something awful, but the sand seemed to have settled out somewhat. I could see now for maybe as much as a hundred feet. I sat up and looked around me. The dirt fell off my shoulders and I shook it out of my hair the way a dog does water. Dust flew. My ears was clogged with it, too.

First thing I did was untangle the barb wire from my person. Even being able to see the coils, it was not easy. I was pretty cut up, but no great damage was done. I stood up and slapped the most of the dirt off me and out of my trousers, surveying the land around me as I done so.

It didn't look nothing like it had before. You couldn't even see the road, for the layer of dirt on everything was six inches to a foot thick. Where fence posts or anything stood up from the ground, there was drifts as deep as three or four feet. It was just like after a snowstorm, only it was dirt.

I was able to find the road again by the ditches that ran either side of it. I stood on the edge and looked both ways, but I couldn't see more than a little distance through the dust, and with the running and turning and tumbling I had done, I didn't have no idea which way Amarillo was supposed to lay. Then I spied the railroad tracks across the way, dusty but standing up out of the dirt, and I got my orientation back. Keeping the tracks on my right, I started along the road toward town. I wondered what would be left of it.

I hadn't gone far when I made out a body hunkered down along the side of the road, and when I got to it, I found it was Monroe. He shot up when he seen me, and grabbed me and held me close and worried me back and forth till I was chafed.

He had been the smart one. When it went black, he had stopped in his tracks. He reached out one way and another for me, but by that time I had bolted — though, naturally, I never told him this — and he couldn't lay a hand on me. So he made his way to the edge of the road, in case some Texas fool should be driving in that storm, and stayed put.

Now he noticed my cuts and said, "What in the Sam Hill happened to you?"

I said, "Oh, nothing much. Let's get out of this damn wind."

It was still blowing quite a gale, though not so bad as what had already passed, and it didn't seem like it was lessening at all. If it should get worse again, I preferred the indoors somewhere.

We picked our way along toward Amarillo, looking for a house or a barn or a storm cellar to hole up in. And now, from behind us, we heard the clack of a train coming. How she dared move in such a storm is beyond me, but I guess since a train didn't do nothing but follow the tracks and since she had a cowcatcher on the front of the engine, she wasn't afraid. Still she was taking it mighty slow, making sure no dust drifts was too deep to plow through.

As she drawed alongside, we seen an empty boxcar. We didn't say a word but went right for it. It was easy enough to board since the train was going so slow. Monroe swung hisself in first, then reached a hand down to me and pulled me up. It was dark inside with dust swirling in eddies stirred up by the wind coming through the doors, but it was a sight better than being out in the open. There was some cardboard in one end, and using that and some lining paper we tore off the walls, we made ourselves a pallet. Then we slid the doors shut to keep the rest of Texas outside where it belonged, and we settled down to wait out the storm.

It wasn't too long before we felt the train come to a stop. We started to slide open the door to see where we was, but the wind screamed into the car carrying more dirt, and we closed it right back up. From the sound of it, the storm was picking up again. We judged we was happy enough where we was.

It's awful boring sitting in a black, closed-up boxcar in a dust storm, and by and by I laid down and took a snooze. So did Monroe. We woke up some time later when we heard a series of bumps and started to move again.

"They're humping us," Monroe said, which meant we was in the train yard and on a siding where the switchers was breaking up the old train and making up new trains. We could hear more humping all around us, and in it all, still the wind howled. Listening to it blow, and as the dust settled in our boxcar, me and Monroe begun to feel right snug. That cardboard and paper pallet didn't seem half bad, and we turned over and dozed again.

We must have got humped three or four times while we laid there, and it did become such a nuisance to our slumber, all that starting and stopping. Pretty soon I got pretty good at not even waking. Then the next thing I knowed, we was moving and still moving.

"Monroe," I said, shaking him awake, "we're going somewhere."

"Good," he said. "If I never see Amarillo again, it will be too soon."

We had to put our bandannas back over our faces because the movement of the train was unsettling the dust in the boxcar again. We choked and choked and choked some more. It was an awful rough ride, and as the train picked up speed we couldn't sit or lie down but had to squat, taking up the bounce with our knees. Monroe said that our car must have been one of a long string of empties to be bumping around so. Usually when you choose a boxcar you try to get a good clean one so the grit don't blow. And if you're lucky, you get one between two loaded boxcars to weight it down and give you the smoothest ride. But with this here rattler we got the worst possible of vehicles, and that ride was pure misery. I got tossed off my squat and onto my tailbone so hard and so often that my bottom become the fixation of my existence.

Some time later, oh, hours and hours it seemed, we didn't hear the wind so much anymore and it grew brighter in the car, the shafts of light coming through the cracks around the door seeming to have more and more substance. We judged we was passing out of the storm and slid open the leeward door. Sure enough, there was the sun shining through the dust, an orange ball just going down, so dim you could look right at it without squinting. But there it was, back again, just the same. The old sun.

Now there was more dust inside the boxcar than outside, so we slid open the other door and encouraged the wind to flood through. We stuck our heads out and shook out our hair and bandannas and took us some pretty good, pretty clean breaths. The countryside laid around us pretty well devastated, the crops buried. Looking back toward Amarillo we could see the backside of that moving mountain range. Well sir, that's the only duster I ever seen, but when I think that that was just one of hundreds that passed through the Dust Bowl, I by turns marvel over the courage of those people who stayed and wonder at the sanity of them.

The sun went down for the second time that day, this time naturally, out in the west where it should. Out in the west where we intended going. And by its position we reckoned now that our train was heading south. Well, that's what you get when you take potluck on your boxcars, a detour. Me and Monroe wasn't worried, though. We wasn't in any particular hurry anymore, now that we had missed the preacher in Tascosa, and we was so pleased at getting out of that duster that we would have detoured all the way to Panama without complaint. So we squatted and rode, and the dark fell. And still the train rolled on.

With the dark come the cold. We closed up the doors again and huddled together to hold what warmth we could. Monroe untied his sooty clothes and give me the shirt to put on over my clothes and tied the trousers over his shoulders. We was now so dirty again that we didn't mind the extra contamination of the coal dust.

We talked it over and couldn't figure out why this train wasn't stopping. It was unlike a manifest to haul a bunch of empties like this, yet a local would have stopped many times over in all these little Texas towns we was passing through. Monroe said it must be heading to pick up a special shipment.

The night lasted a couple of eternities with us rocking over the land. I got better at the squat, keeping my balance and saving my tailbone. But in a night that long, a squat gets mighty hard on the joints, I tell you. Then finally, just before daylight, we come to a stop in a regular pandemonium.

Before we slid open the door, we could already tell that we was in the middle of a herd of cattle, only it sounded like a couple dozen herds of cattle. The bellowing and stamping was something dreadful. Then when we opened the doors and in the growing light of dawn saw them thousands of head of sharp and swishing longhorns, the sight was even more dreadful.

There was a lot of people out there too, milling around, carrying cattle ramps, herding the cattle, or waving papers in the air, and all of them shouting to and at each other and the cows. Me and Monroe opened up the other door. It was clearer on this side of the train and we could get off without being trampled. Looking back, we seen now that the train was a cattle train and that most of the cars was slat-sided cattle cars. Ours was one of only a half dozen or so boxcars. And every single car was empty.

"Where do you suppose they're taking all these cows?" I said to Monroe. He just shook his head in wonder.

Now in Atoka, I had seen cows of course, but never so many at once. This here took my breath away. Me and Monroe wandered about among the chaos, not knowing just what to do or where to go. We could hear deals being made all around us. There was appraisers and there was owners and there was ranch hands. As the appraisers and owners haggled and come to agreement, the ranch hands cut out animal after animal, dividing them into three groups. The best of the cattle was chuted one by one up the ramps onto the cattle cars. The middling animals — that is, them that seemed too poorly to be shipped but not so bad they couldn't be ate — was herded off to what, by the look and smell of it, was a slaughterhouse. The least animals, and they was awful sorry beasts, was herded off to I didn't care to think where.

As me and Monroe loitered around gawking, I come to be aware of someone watching us. She was a handsome woman of middle age with a flash in her eye and with her dark hair piled up after the fashion of women who mean business. It was the way Mama always put up her hair when she was fixing to whip me. This woman, after gazing at us for some minutes, making me mighty nervous I can tell you, seemed to come to some decision about us and come bearing down on us with a full head of steam. I pulled on Monroe's shirtsleeve and was making ready to run when she hailed us.

"You boys," she said, and after that I could no sooner have run than flown. She had just the loveliest voice. I can't describe anything about it but the texture, which was just like honey, and the cadence, which was just the way a fine saddle horse breaks into a short lope. It wasn't just, "You boys," the way anyone else would say it; it was more like, "You-uh boys-uh," with ever so many sweet little extra sounds to it. I hadn't ever heard anyone talk so lovely.

I found out later that she was from Italy and her name was Eleonora Landover. She had been a great opera singer in Europe before she married Ira Landover of Filigree, Texas, who saw her on the stage in London and wouldn't come home to the Lone Star State until she had consented to be his bride. He had told her he was a cattle baron *and* an oil tycoon, but in point of fact he was little better than a free-thinking dirt farmer with a taste for the elegant. How was she to know until she come to Filigree and seen the Landover "estate" that she had been hoodwinked? But by that time she was pregnant with her first child, and besides, she was in love with the man.

"Yes, ma'am?" Monroe said to her.

"You come through that duster up north, huh?" she said, only like I said, with lots more honey to it. She looked us up and down, and I was awful aware of just exactly how dirty we was. "You look hungry," she said. "Do you want work?"

Me and Monroe looked at each other, and he answered, "Yes, ma'am, I reckon we do."

She said, "Good. I'll feed you and give you seventy-five cents for the day and the little one fifty cents. If that is acceptable, come with me."

Even in those days, it was piss-poor pay, but we wasn't going to argue. She turned and walked toward the slaughterhouse on the other side of the train yard. Me and Monroe followed, me almost running to keep up with her. Inside the building, there was sides of beef hanging from meat hooks all along the walls. A crew of men worked behind long counters hacking and sawing at the meat, throwing fat and bone into piles on the floor. The stink of blood was strong, and my stomach, empty and mistreated as it was, come near revolting.

The lady went up to a man behind one of the counters and said, "I'll take as much as you'll give me."

He looked at her askance and then wrapped up some largish chunks of meat in butcher paper and pushed them across the counter at her.

She said, "May I cut my own?"

He said, "No, Mrs. Landover, I'm sorry but you can't. These is our jobs, and we want to keep them."

She said, "Very well, then, may I select my own cuts?"

He said, "No, ma'am. This here's relief food. We cut it. We choose it. Because we give it. This ain't your butcher shop, Mrs. Landover."

She didn't say nothing for a long moment. Then she said, "Very well."

They looked at each other a moment, until finally he pointed to the wrapped meat in front of her and said, "There's your meat, Mrs. Landover."

"Yes," she said. "I'd like more, please."

He give her another of those looks, then wrapped up one more chunk, a goodly piece, as they all was, and pushed it across to her. She waited. He waited. She waited more. Then he wrapped up one last piece and pushed it at her.

"That's it," he said.

She said, "I am not aware that the Emergency Relief Committee set any limits on the amount of meat per person."

"The Emergency Relief Committee didn't," the man said. "God did. And the amount you got there is gluttonous, Mrs. Landover."

"Did God tell you that personally, Mr. Johnson? If not, why don't you leave that judgment to God, and give me the meat I ask for?"

He went very red. By now, all the butchers around him had laid aside their cleavers and saws and had moved to a quieter kind of slicing so as not to miss a word.

The man said, "I got a responsibility to the citizens of Filigree to divide up this meat equal."

Mrs. Landover looked behind her pointedly and said, "Where are these citizens, Mr. Johnson, who are lining up for this free meat?"

He leaned across the counter at her and sneered, "They're at home in their beds. I don't suppose any but a greedy Eye-talian *would* be out this early scavenging."

She never even blinked but said, "Mr. Johnson, you say you want to keep your job. I will be glad to report to the committee that I came here, requested relief, and was denied relief, even though no one else was applying for that relief."

"What do you mean 'no one else'?" he said, pointing to Monroe and me. "Here are some young men right here. You want meat, boys?" he said, grinning at us. "Here." And he wrapped chunk after chunk after chunk of meat and pushed them at us, all the time leering at Mrs. Landover. He seen we was dirty. He must have knowed we wasn't from Filigree. Yet he heaped all that meat on us where it was bound to go to waste rather than bow to Mrs. Landover.

Me and Monroe never said a word but hauled the meat to our side of the counter. Mrs. Landover watched it pass with a keen eye. Finally she give a little signal to Monroe, and Monroe said to the man, "Thank you very much. I think this will do me just fine."

Then we both picked up an armful and went out the door. Mrs. Landover followed in a few seconds, carrying her packages of meat. She pointed to the wagon yard to a neat, newly painted little hack with a blue roan pony in the harness and said, "Put it in there, and quick, run back and get the rest."

Me and Monroe made several more trips back into the building until we got the rest of the meat loaded into the bed of the hack. Then Monroe took his place next to her on the seat, and I got in the back with the meat. She clucked to the pony and slapped the reins, and he trotted off.

The town of Filigree fell behind us without much notice. It wasn't much of a town. The country hereabouts was still pretty flat, but there was a nice little hill here and there to give you the feeling that there was a reason to go over it. There was more water here, too, than up north in the Panhandle. We crossed over a couple of good-sized cricks on the way.

This here was cattle country, and great big. But hither and yon among the pastures was tucked smaller farms growing cotton, corn, and sorghum. Though the cotton had a month to six weeks' growth on it, it wasn't looking like a good cotton season in these parts.

Monroe said, just trying to make conversation, you know, "That's a good-looking little pony you got there."

"Yes," she said. "I'd show horses with the President."

I liked this woman. Squatting behind her and Monroe — my tailbone was too bruised for sitting, I tell you — watching the sunburned nape of her neck, the way the hair was combed up from it neat, and the way the muscles in her neck slid about under the skin as she worked the reins, I had time to do some reflecting. Mama had told me about Italians, or "Eye-talians," as she always called them. Hearing from Mr. Johnson in the slaughterhouse that Mrs. Landover was one of them was a real shock to me. She just didn't fit the picture.

First of all, Italians was supposed to be colored. Or at least I always imagined them to be colored because Mama always put them on the yonder side of the color line, referring to Negroes, Indians, Mexicans, and Eye-talians as "them" as opposed to "us" white folk. Second of all, Italians was supposed to be dirty. Yet here was me and Monroe, as dirty as all Texas, and here was Mrs. Landover, as clean and starched as table linens. Last of all, Italians was supposed to be all Catholics, and there wasn't nothing worse in Mama's book but only Satan.

"Are you a Catholic?" I said, leaning in between Monroe and Mrs. Landover to get a better look at her. Monroe give me a jab in the ribs with his elbow.

Mrs. Landover turned to me and said, "Who wants to know?"

I said, "Blue Roan of Atoka, Oklahoma."

She said, "You got the name of a horse, Blue Roan."

"Yes, ma'am."

"Are you a horse?"

I didn't answer right up because the question seemed

to me more than a little impertinent. More than that, the answer seemed to me more than a little obvious. I wondered if she had thought the same about my question. But the more I thought about it, the more I thought about it. And finally I said, "No, ma'am. Are you a Catholic or not?"

Monroe's elbow give me another jab that about broke my ribcage. But Mrs. Landover laughed. It was a musical sort of laugh, and it just give me the shivers to hear it. She said, "No. Not anymore."

I said, "What are you then?"

I seen Monroe start with his elbow again and I turned quick and said, "Monroe! Would you stop that!"

Mrs. Landover laughed again.

Monroe said, "Well, you stop, Blue! The lady's gone think we got no upbringing!"

I said, "The lady's name is Mrs. Landover, and her and me is talking!" I turned back to Mrs. Landover and said, "Mrs. Landover, I'd like to apologize for the way that man treated you back there."

She looked at me again, and her look was strange. She said, "Why should you apologize for him?"

I puzzled over this a moment, then said, "I don't rightly know. But it seems I should."

She smiled then, and it was worth gold to me, and she said, "Thank you, then, for your apology." She clucked to the pony, which had begun to lag, showing a toothy kind of interest in a patch of lamb's quarters growing along the roadside. And we moved on.

Eight

"WHEN DID YOU BOYS last eat?" Mrs. Landover said as we pulled up before her house. It wasn't much of a house from the outside, a smallish frame house with two stories, an attic and a basement, but it had a new coat of white-wash and looked in good repair. And inside, every room was newly papered and just as pretty as a picture. All around the house lay the land, as good as any farm I ever come across. Mrs. Landover growed cotton, and she knowed what she was about. It wasn't the straggling, weevil-ridden cotton we had seen along the way, but a good, healthy crop that was going to come in well.

"Well, ma'am," Monroe allowed, "we ain't had nothing to eat for a little while now."

I was more exact. "Not since yesterday morning," I said, "and that was nothing but an old, woody turnip."

"First things first, then," she said. She showed us to her bathroom, to her own bathroom, with a porcelain tub and toilet just sparkling white. She give us soap and towels and said, "Use all the water you need. My well is deep and never runs dry. I'll fire up the stove and you'll have hot water soon."

She said it with pride. She had reason for it because this was about the best outfitted little farmhouse I ever seen. Even in town in those days not all the houses was modernized with running water. But this woman not only had running water, but hot running water to boot. She had a fair-sized water tank built on stilts on a rise nearby which provided a gravity flow into the house, through copper coils in the wood stove, and up to the second story to the bathtub. She had a septic tank out back that it all run out into. Just a jim-dandy little homestead.

Well sir, you can imagine how me and Monroe luxuriated in that bath. We washed and washed and washed and sent so much mud down that drain, I feared we'd plug it. Then we washed again and got a fair semblance of clean, though it was over a week before I got all the grit out of my scalp.

Mrs. Landover give us some temporary clothes and some soap flakes to wash our own clothes, which we did in an old Maytag in a washroom outside the kitchen, putting them through the wringer into good concrete stationary tubs. Then we went in to eat. Mrs. Landover checked my hands and give me a look that said they wasn't good enough, so I went back to the bathroom and washed again, with Monroe right behind me. We didn't neither of us pass the second test either, so back again. If you've never tried to get dirt out from under your fingernails after a duster and an all-nighter in a boxcar, then you don't know.

Finally both me and Monroe passed the cleanliness test,

and Mrs. Landover sat us down to about the best breakfast I ever ate.

Now at first I have to say that I had my reservations. Mama had always told me, "Chinamen eat cats, Mexicans eat dogs, and Eye-talians eat worms." So I was anything but eager to sit down to Mrs. Landover's table. But what she set before us was the best of what Mama ever cooked: bacon, and there was no question but it was real pig; eggs, and we all know where they come from; and good milk gravy over biscuits. Me and Monroe ate to surfeit, Mrs. Landover waiting on us like she and not us was the hired help.

After breakfast, though, we went to work, and I guess I never spent a busier day. We hauled that meat into the kitchen and set about cutting it up. Mrs. Landover clucked and tsked and talked in Italian, shaking her head all the while, and I could tell she was irked over the way the butchers had cut up the meat.

"Look at this!" she said once in English. "A beautiful 'something-or-other-in-Italian' ruined by those butchers!"

None of the meat was much good, and she complained of that, too. I didn't know nothing about it then, but now that I have growed my own beeves for food, I know that you got to grain-feed your animal in that last month before the slaughter. This marbles the fat into the meat and makes it tender and juicy. But this here relief meat had come from those middling cows, and it was awful lean and stringy.

There wasn't much Mrs. Landover could do to correct most of the cuts, and that meat she assigned to hamburger, and me she assigned to the grinder. Some of the better cuts of meat she assigned for smoking, and Monroe she assigned to the smokehouse, chopping wood and keeping a good smoky fire going. Other cuts she put into a barrel of brine for corning. Still other chunks of meat she had Monroe cut into small, bitey pieces, and these she canned in a pressure cooker, quart after quart which we carried out to the tidiest little stone storm cellar you ever seen, lined with shelves of canned fruit and vegetables and now meat, all labeled in a tight, clean hand. Why, there was food in there to last a family a year or more.

Mama always said, "An Eye-talian never lets a nickel slip through," and I guess maybe in that one way she was right about Mrs. Landover. I never seen such a home economist.

As we worked, sharing the kitchen, I asked a lot of questions, and Mrs. Landover was very free in answering. She explained about the cattle and slaughterhouse. It was a part of President Roosevelt's relief plan, she said. The cattlemen in this area was having a hard time of it. There was too many cattle and not enough buyers. The cattle was overgrazing the range so that there wasn't no grass anymore to keep the wind from blowing away the soil. Though it wasn't so bad here as up in the Panhandle, it soon could be. The cows had to be got rid of, and fast. So the feds stepped in and set up this relief program where they bought the cattle off the farmers at a fair, or pretty fair, price. They shipped the best of them off to packing companies nationwide, at once creating jobs and distributing the canned meat for relief. Those folks in the cities was having it hard, too, and I guess that canned meat was awful welcome to them. Meanwhile the herds of cattle was reduced, helping the pastures to grow back some of their grass cover.

I asked why more people wasn't down to the slaughter-house picking up their free meat. Mrs. Landover snorted.

"These people!" she said. "They don't know. 'Next year . . . Next year,' they say. Well, next year I'm ready. But where will they be?"

She took the hamburger meat I had ground and started frying it, sending me first to the garden to gather what few tomatoes had already ripened this early in the season, and then to the storm cellar for quarts of last year's toma-toes. She made a vat of meat sauce she said was for spaghetti, and then ladled it into quart jars, and pressure-cooked them. These too, after they cooled, we took back out to the storm cellar.

I kept looking for Mr. Landover to show up, but I guessed he went out to the fields early. Around about 9:00 in the morning, a girl showed herself at the kitchen door, still in her nightgown, her hair all dripping down over her shoulders. Even though she was nearly Monroe's age, she didn't show any sign of embarrassment at appearing before us in this outfit, but gapped and stretched and rubbed her eyes, her pointy breasts raising up under the thin cloth.

"Morning, Ma," she said. Then she turned to us. "Morning, you two."

It was strange to hear her talk just like one of us. Maybe I expected her to have her mother's same soft accent, I don't know. I looked over to Monroe, and he was just agog, his eyes swimming all over them breasts of hers.

Mrs. Landover quit her work and fixed the girl breakfast, calling her honey and dear and just spoiling her something terrible. The girl ate it all up and went back upstairs.

Then about 10:00 a boy about my age come down the stairs, and him too in his nightshirt, gapping and rubbing his eyes. Mrs. Landover quit her work and fixed his breakfast and honeyed him, too. He was runty like me, and blanched in the skin like he never seen the light of day. He sat across the table opposite where I stood grinding the meat. I smiled, but he didn't. He wore the expression of a grub just dug out of its log and stuck on a fishhook.

My right arm was getting awful tired, and I said to him, like it was going to be fun, "You want to grind some?"

He said, "I wouldn't mind, I guess." But he looked to his mother and she shook her head.

Then she said to me, "Ira has to take care of his hands. He is going to be a concert pianist."

Well sir, at first I thought she said something else, and I went just hot with embarrassment. But later I found out she meant that he had to save his hands to play the piano.

Neither Ira nor Mary, as I found out his sister was named, did a lick of work that day. In fact, they didn't do nothing but go into one or another room and practice one or another musical instrument, hour in hour out. Ira punched a piano in the parlor, going up and down the scales, and nothing else, until I about went stark nuts. Meanwhile, Mary was somewhere upstairs sawing out scales of her own on a squawky fiddle, and such a racket you never heard.

But Mrs. Landover, she nodded the while and smiled, only every occasionally raising her eyebrows like she was

95

jabbed. Then she'd wash her hands and dry them and disappear for a few minutes. The piano would stop, or the violin, and you'd hear her musical voice giving some kind of instruction. Then she'd come back to the kitchen and the scales would resume. I never knowed such a tediousness.

I said to Mrs. Landover, "Don't they know any songs?"

She said, "Oh yes. But technique is everything."

I didn't say nothing, though I had my disagreements.

We didn't finish processing all that meat until the sun was nearly down. Still Mr. Landover didn't come home from the fields. Mrs. Landover give us our pay, six bits for Monroe and four bits for me, just like she said, and sat us down at the kitchen table and fed us. Smelling her spaghetti sauce cooking all day had made me most faint with hunger, so I was awful pleased when I seen that was the very food she was intending to feed us.

However, I had never seen spaghetti before. Oh, I had seen it raw, in packages in stores, without knowing what it was called. But I had never guessed what it looked like cooked. So now, when Mrs. Landover dished it up out of that boiling water, and I seen it pale and squirmy on the plate, I understood why Mama had told me what she had about Eye-talians and worms. It pretty well gagged me.

Mrs. Landover sat down with us to eat, having already fed Mary and Ira in the dining room, and when I seen her twisting those strands of spaghetti into that blood-red sauce, I like to swoon. I looked over to Monroe and seen he was diving into his plate just that same way. I guess he had already met up with Italians somewhere on the tracks, because he didn't show no signs of holding back. I picked

96

up my knife and fork but, try as I might, couldn't bring that mess anywhere near my mouth.

Then I seen Mrs. Landover looking over at me with a smile. "You think it's worms," she said. I couldn't think of nothing to say to that. And now Monroe looked up at me and just howled. "It's flour and egg and water," she said. "You just take a bite."

So finally, trusting her, I did take a bite. And I don't suppose I ever ate anything tastier.

"The day I arrived in New York," Mrs. Landover said to me, smiling again, "my husband bought me a sandwich from one of the vendors on the dock. It was so delicious! After eating half of it, I asked him what kind of meat it was. He told me hot dog. So you see, Blue, I know how you feel."

We helped Mrs. Landover clean up the kitchen and then made ready to go our way, our work for her done. I was feeling a little raw about leaving because I had so enjoyed the day and so admired the woman. And where was there to go to so darn fast anymore? After those freights, it was good to settle down with such amiable company as Mrs. Landover. Maybe, too, I was a little homesick for Mama, and though Mrs. Landover wasn't a thing like Mama, she warmed me the way Mama always done.

Mrs. Landover said, "You boys do good work. I like you."

"Thank you, ma'am," Monroe said.

"How would you like to work again tomorrow?"

I said, "You ain't got no more jars for canning, Mrs. Landover."

She said, "No, the meat is done. Tomorrow, I'm planting trees."

"Trees?" Monroe laughed. "If God couldn't plant trees on these plains, Mrs. Landover, you can't."

"Maybe God didn't want to, Monroe," she said. "I do."

Monroe didn't say nothing, but just grinned like a dumb dog and wagged his head.

"What do you say, boys?" she said. "And now that I know your work, I'll pay you more. A dollar apiece. No more kid's pay for Blue; he works like a man."

I said yes, right off. But Monroe, he hesitated. Just then Mary stuck her head in at the door to say goodnight to her Mama. She was looking awful pretty now that she had combed her hair and put on a dress. The next minute, Monroe, he said yes, too.

Mrs. Landover took us out to a tarpaper shanty which stood out back of the house. There was electricity strung to it, and inside, it was just as neat as a pin, though the mattress on the bed was bare.

"Will you sleep together?" Mrs. Landover asked, and we said, oh yes. She brought us out fresh sheets and pillows and a multitude of blankets, and presently it begun to look just fine out there. I never seen a bed more inviting.

She pointed to the outhouse we were to use and said that in the morning we could come inside to wash up again. She left us alone then. I undressed as fast as ever I did, and when my head hit my pillow, it was already asleep.

Nine

THE PLANTING OF THE TREES was another relief project from Franklin Delano Roosevelt. He thought, and he was right, that if there was trees on the Great Plains, a great long "Shelterbelt" that extended from Texas all the way up to Canada, then moisture would be held in the ground, and the winds would be broke up, saving the soil from blowing off.

Well, didn't those farmers give that notion the hoo-haw! Just like Monroe did to Mrs. Landover, they just wagged their heads and grinned.

But Mrs. Landover was right behind the President. She leased a strip of land all around her farm to the government, promising to plant it with young trees which government nurseries provided her. In return the government give her a few dollars per acre and hired her to do her own plowing and fencing and cultivating of the trees. She in turn hired me and Monroe.

That was good, sandy soil she had on that farm, and well tended, so there wasn't nothing to the plowing of it.

Not like Preacher Starr's land in Atoka, so full of roots and stumps that you like to bust a gut on both you and the plowhorse.

When we went into town in Mrs. Landover's hack to pick up the seedling trees, you should have heard those townspeople hoot. But Mrs. Landover, she didn't pay them no mind, and we made trip after trip. There must have been about a dozen varieties of trees we was to plant, and those government nurserymen was good and helpful in telling us just how to do it. They was facing the derision of a whole nation of people, so when folks like Mrs. Landover was cooperative, they was real cooperative back. And after Mrs. Landover took it up, and those seedlings looked so hardy and neat, some of the other farmers come in and took it up too. Seems like that's always the way of it. Sheep need a good ram to follow.

We planted the tallest varieties in the center of the strip, and the shrubbier stuff along the edges, the idea being to lift the wind and get it back up in the air where it belonged, and off the land. Now, watering them seedlings was a problem, but I guess Mrs. Landover could tackle about any problem she needed to. She had that good well and that little water tower of hers, and she rigged up an awful clever irrigation system, and I reckon there wasn't a tree among the lot that didn't survive.

Years later during the Second World War, I come back through this area as a soldier boy, shipped home on leave, and all around this area those Shelterbelt trees we planted was growing tall and green. The land was prime again. It give me the shivers, seeing it, seeing that land recovering from such bad times. But then I heard some years after that the farmers begun to get greedy again as the times got better. They didn't see no profit in them acres of trees, and they cut them down and plowed the land. And sure enough, come some dry years in the fifties, and that whole area turned to dust bowl again. You would think, wouldn't you, that mankind could learn just some little something from history. But no.

And that's another story.

Now, during the time me and Monroe and Mrs. Landover was planting these Shelterbelt trees, I decided to satisfy my curiosities about Eleonora Landover. I took aside Ira-Grub, as me and Monroe called him in private, and questioned him as to where the absentee Mr. Landover was.

"My daddy's in his grave," he said.

I was vexed to hear it. I had such a feeling for Mrs. Landover that I wanted the best for her, and a dead husband didn't fit. It seems, though, that Mr. Landover died a hero, at least in the eyes of his family.

"They shot him!!" Ira-Grub said, his eyes just bugging out of his head.

"Who did?"

"People from town."

"Who?"

"I don't know. They was wearing hoods."

"Why'd they shoot him?"

"Because he was a Free Thinker."

"Well, just how free was his thinking?"

"He married a wop, didn't he?"

Well, I about laid him low right there. "Don't you talk about your Mama that way!" I said to him.

"She's my Mama! I guess I can talk about her any way I want to!"

"Not in front of me! Not and stay standing!"

He backed down. Of course I knew he would. I never seen such a kid without backbone as that Ira-Grub.

"What's a wop?" I said to him.

"I don't know. That's what they call her in town."

"Is that why they shot your Daddy?"

"No. He was a unionizer!"

Now Mama had told me all about womanizers, her every husband but the first and last having been one, but until this moment with Ira-Grub I had never heard tell of a unionizer.

"What's that?" I said.

Ira-Grub run me out a long story, over half of which I judged to be the baldest of lies, all about how his Daddy had tried to organize a union called Sharecroppers and Tenant Farmers of Texas, and how he had even been invited to Washington, D.C., to meet with President Roosevelt. Though Mr. Landover owned his farm hisself, and was proud of it, he had compassion for the farmers who couldn't afford their own land but had to rent it. These folks was really down. And that's how the landowners wanted to keep them.

Now, the feds at this time, because of there being no market for crops, was paying landowners not to plant certain acres of their farms. Well, that was just fine for the landowners, to get money for letting their land lay fallow. But the sharecroppers and tenant farmers, who was mostly black, couldn't live if their acres was retired. Mr. Landover, seeing this, was trying to get them to band together.

It was beyond me just exactly what they was intending to do once they was organized. But I guess Mr. Landover had a plan.

In any case, one night a bunch of men in white robes and hoods drove out to the Landover farm. Mr. Landover must've knowed what was going to happen because he made Mrs. Landover and Mary and Ira-Grub go up to their bedrooms when he answered the door. Ira-Grub heard three shots. Then he heard his Mama scream and the car drive away.

"Downstairs," Ira-Grub said — and I could tell by the way his face was pinched that this part of the story was all truth — "I found my Mama standing over my Daddy in a puddle of blood. The top of his head was blowed off, and his brains and bits of bone and hair was running down the wall behind him."

Well sir, after this story I looked at Mrs. Landover with new eyes. That a woman, a foreign woman who got nothing but jeers and hatred from her neighbors, should abide even after they killed her husband, and in such a way . . . Well, the woman just had to be crazy. There wasn't no other explanation.

That was my first thought. Then I thought again. Here she was, alone with two children to rear, and a piece of property which those children called home. She could uproot them. Or she could abide.

Well, as I said before, she was a handsome woman.

I guess I doubled my output for her when I heard Ira-Grub's story, though I was never what you'd call a sluggard in any case. After we got them acres of trees planted, she approached us as to whether we might not like to stay on longer, because she was proud of our work. It was time to chop the cotton — that is, chop the weeds back from between and among the cotton plants. She apologized she couldn't pay us more, because there was a deal of work to be done and she could use two hands like us all year round. But there was the problem of money. Well, now that I knowed her adversity, I would have stayed on for free. I just felt awful sad for her.

When she paid me for the planting of the seedlings, it was for the whole week's work, and it did seem a heap of money to be taking away from her. I tried to give half of it back, saying it was for my room and board, but she looked at me a long time like I was a crazy boy, and pressed my fingers closed around them bills, never saying a word.

The cotton chopping was easy because of the careful way the field had been planted and plowed. With Mrs. Landover working beside us — and it was ever so hard to keep up with her row after row; I never seen such a hand with a hoe — the three of us finished the whole crop, I'd say a good forty acres, in less than a week.

I said, "Are you going to get Ira and Mary to help you pick this cotton when it comes in?"

She said, "Oh no! It'd ruin their hands."

I nodded my head. That's what I thought her answer would be. Two more spoiled kids would be hard to find in the state of Texas. Picking cotton was about the bloodiest job I knowed, and so far, I hadn't heard nothing but scales coming off them pampered fingertips.

The barn and a couple of the outbuildings needed a little attention, and me and Monroe stayed an extra day and put them to rights. And then we was ready to move on, though both of us was feeling awful heavy.

Monroe had begun feeling pangs of something he called love for Mary, even though she was about as sassy a girl as I ever hoped to meet, and never cast Monroe a second glance. I kept telling him to remember Marge, and when that didn't seem to stir him, to at least remember Rose Jewel and Violet Ruby. But the only Starrs he could see was the ones in the Texas sky shining down on the hair of Mary Landover.

On the night of our last day, Mary and Ira both was to perform on violin and piano in a musicale called "Heartstrings of Texas" over at the Corbett homestead. I wouldn't have dreamed of attending because if ever in my life I had wished to sit down and listen to scales, I had already had that wish come too true. To anyone but Mrs. Landover I'd have give the horse laugh. But she was so sweet when she extended to us her invitation that I lost my head.

"It's our last night together, boys," she said. "Tomorrow I suppose you'll be on those tracks again."

Monroe allowed we would be, though I could tell it hurt him to think of leaving his unrequited love behind, and still ever so unrequited.

She said, "If you'd like, I would be very pleased if you could come tonight to our musicale. I know that you have not been invited, but my family has been invited, and you are like family to me now."

So you see, even though it had all the makings of being just a dismal evening, I wouldn't have said no for nothing. Mrs. Landover brought us out some good, fancy duds, a second suit of Ira's for me, and what I'm sure was a suit of her husband's for Monroe. She didn't explain, but just handed it over to Monroe, without so much as a tear in her eye. I'd never seen either of us in a suit before, and if I do say so who says it, with our hair slicked and our cheeks fresh-scrubbed, we looked like quality gentry stepping into that Corbett parlor.

Mrs. Corbett was a plump, shortish woman with a face just like that on a sow we had in Atoka named Pinky. Her little nose upturned so you could see right up her nostrils. Her eyes was squinty and just lost behind her chubby cheeks. And her ears was even a little pointy. Her given name was Susie, and I had the hardest time not laughing when I was introduced to her because I remembered just as though I was hearing it Mama's hogcall, "Sooey!"

But Mrs. Corbett was as nice as she could be, welcoming Monroe and me as though our invitations was engraved. Her husband was a distinguished-looking man of about fifty-five, with hair graying at the temples and a face lined and scarred with years of work among the elements. He shook my hand with a grip so strong I had to grit my teeth to keep from hollering. I have since learned to distrust a man who feels he must greet you so severe, because most generally he is a man afraid.

There wasn't nobody else at the musicale, just the Corbetts and the Landovers and Monroe and me. If others was invited, they declined. Small talk was made, and I'd say the weather come up fifty to one more often than any other subject. We talked it first this way, then that, and then the other. I felt me and Monroe had the corner on the market, having just come through two storms you could list in a book of records, but Mr. Corbett was the kind of man who would not be bested. By the end of the night, he was telling about a duster he survived that stretched from the Rockies to the Mississippi. I allowed to myself that this was a stretcher indeed, but I knowed to keep quiet.

My, but couldn't the man talk, though! One topic he leapt upon had me just trembling in my shoes at first for fear of offense to Mrs. Landover. He kept on and on about "the colored problem," and what was to be done about it. Now, though he specified he meant Negroes — only he said it "Niggroes," as though he would go only so far and no further — I remembered again that Mama always referred to Italians as colored. So I kept myself ready to fly to Mrs. Landover's side in case she was attacked. But she didn't seem to mind Mr. Corbett's talk.

"Now the reason we're in this here Depression," Mr. Corbett was saying, swelling up and gesticulating so grand that an octopus couldn't have outdone him, "is because of the Niggro population in this country. It's as plain as the nose on your face, and any fool can see it what has eyes in his head. We got this much food" (here he made a little bitty gesture like he was piling up a little bitty stack) "and we got this much people" (here he made a great big gesture like he was piling up a great big stack) "and any fool with any brains of any kind can see that there ain't enough food in that little pile to feed all them people. And so we got to get rid of the Niggro!

"Now the Niggro has a very good home over there in Africa," he went right on without paying any of us the least mind, which seemed just about all the mind he had

107

to pay. "And so why don't the Niggro just go on home, and leave the white man our country?

"Now I talked once with a Niggro who said . . . and he was a good Niggro, knowed his place . . . who said all he wanted to do was see his homeland, that his yearning for Africa was so deep that he could not lay down his head and die before he had earned his passage . . . and he said earned! He was willing to work for it! Yessir, he was a good Niggro . . . *earned* his passage on a ship bound for the Black Continent.

"And so, if that numbskull in Washington had a particle of the brains in his head that I've got in the dirt under the fingernail of my little finger, instead of these WPAs and PWAs and all the other A's he's spending the taxpayers' money on, he'd hire a fleet of ships . . . each ship with a crew pulling down a living wage, mind you! . . . and he'd ship the Niggro to his beloved homeland and, believe you me, we'd see an end to this godforsaken Depression before the year is out."

My mind went right to my friends Alfay and Omeega Lincoln, two colored boys I played ball with back in Atoka. Them along with Tad Daily, who was a white boy, and a great tall Cherokee Indian, who went by only the one name Cloud, and me formed a baseball team which we called the Breeds. Nobody else would join up with us, I guess because of our mixed colors, but we didn't need only just us five because we whipped every nine-boy team in the county. Tad could pitch a ball that just boggled a batter. Alfay and Omeega played the outfield, right center and left center, and there wasn't a ball hit to any field that got past them. Cloud played shortstop and I played both first and second base. Mama had sewed me a mitt out of a cast-off pair of blue denim jeans, and being so fast in the legs, I could field a ball at second and run the batter out at first with hairs left over. At bat, Cloud could hit a ball a country mile, so we always put him up fourth, having loaded the bases, and still having one man left over to cheer us in at home plate.

Now, Alfay and Omeega was the only two coloreds I knowed much about because in those days the separate peoples kept more separate than they seem to do today. But I had a hard time swallowing that Alfay and Omeega was just dying to get over to Africa, nor that they was in any way the cause of the U.S. Depression, Mr. Corbett's say-so or no.

I was now alone with the man, everyone else having found any little excuse to be drug away, so I don't believe a person there but me was privileged to hear his philosophy. I looked around for a way out myself.

Mrs. Landover had turned her attention to Ira-Grub's tie and the bows in Mary's hair. Ira and Mary was busy making a dozen little last-minute adjustments to just everything they could lay their hands on around their little stage.

With them was the Corbett girl, April May, who was to play the cello in the musicale. April May's hair was so full and wavy, and her face so round and dimpled and creamy, that from the neck up she looked copied out of a movie magazine. But otherwise she was a bony, fragile, little thing with great big hands that never ceased fidgeting, and she hauled along her cello every step she took.

Mrs. Corbett was spreading herself around, having

brought out some of the daintiest little no-nothing bits of refreshment, saying to everyone, "Won't you have a horse dove?" and "Here's a little horse dove, if you'll have it," and all the while her just shoveling them horse doves in, talking around them, bits of them flying out her mouth, so you was constant on the duck.

Monroe, he didn't have eyes nor ears for no one but Mary. That is, until April May come into the room with her cello. And then, April May just as beauteous and delicate as a preened feather, poor Monroe couldn't drag his eyes off her.

Mary seen her danger at once. Though she had made it plain in every possible way on every possible occasion just how far below herself she considered Monroe to be, still, now that his head was turning ever so surely away from her to April May, there wasn't a trick she didn't play to turn it back.

"Oh, Monroe!" she said, and I don't guess there was ever syrup poured any thicker. "Could you help me with my violin case? I seem to have jammed it. Oh, I'm such a silly!"

The littlest Corbett was a toddler named Tally who was carrying around just the limpest old tabby tomcat, weaving her way among all those grownup legs, her eyes wide open looking up at you with all her innocence still intact. The tom's eyes was squeezed tight shut, but every once in a while he'd let go a yowl which showed his terror. It is the most remarkable thing about the fearsome, raging cat, how it will suffer a child to so abuse it without offering a scratch.

So, you see, when Mr. Corbett made his wrap-up on the

Niggro, there was no one but me still attending. I said to him, "Well, that sounds just bully, Mr. Corbett."

But he didn't hear. He was already formulating his next thought, such as it was. I wondered how a smart woman like Mrs. Landover could bear him as a friend, or a sweet woman like Mrs. Corbett bear him as a husband. But I guess in her loneliness an outcast will take what she can get. And some have said, though I have my disagreements, that any husband is better than no husband. But it seems to me more generous to think that it was the music which drawed them all together.

And here come the music. Mrs. Corbett shoveled away what was left of her dainties and directed us to our seats. Mr. Corbett presided in his own special armchair. Mrs. Corbett pulled aside for herself a straight-backed, spindly, torturous-looking, gewgaw of a chair that looked like it would break under her. And Mrs. Landover and Monroe and me took the settee.

"I will now introduce our dear musicians," Mrs. Corbett said, and went on to introduce them, though there was only just the three, Mary, Ira, and April May, and there wasn't a person in the room who wasn't kin or hadn't already met them. They come in and bowed, looking just splendid and flushed, and then they sat down with their instruments, and placed their music on their music stands and turned pages and cleared throats and plucked on this string and that string and did just about everything they could to stretch the moment. Then finally, they was off.

Well sir, I had no preparation at all. I don't know if I expected to hear a lot of scales, or if I expected to hear songs, or what. But I didn't hear neither. It was just the purest music, and it just flooded that room and about lifted off the ceiling. Mary and April May, sawing their violin and cello, was so perfectly together they might have been playing out of one brain. And such a lovely, aching sound they did wring from those strings. And such fire in their eyes. I didn't look at Monroe, him sitting by my side, but I could feel him quiver just like he was one of the catguts the girls was sawing.

On the floor, Tally sat with her tom, whose yowls blent right in with those strings, making it all even mournfuller. I wondered if he sensed his ultimate kinship to the music.

Ira, at the piano, was a changed being. In the trio with Mary and April May, he sat on the edge of the piano bench punching his keys ever so lightly, ever so just right to give a frame for the girls' notes to hang on. He kept his eyes closed for the most of it, rocking and swaying and lilting, like he was dreaming the sound out of the piano.

They played on and on, with me just in raptures, and when they come to the end — this little soft, sweet ending which about broke my heart, the quiet settling over us like a sheet thrown in the air and drifting back down, wrapping us up ever so gently — why, realizing suddenly that it was over, I jumped to my feet with a whoop and begun clapping. Well, the rest of them looked up at me like I had messed my pants. So there was nothing to do but shut up and sit back down. I did feel awful sheepish though. It seemed to me like such musicianship should get some applause, and in Atoka we'd have give it without let-up.

Ira and Mary and April May turned their pages, and it was just lovely to see them do it, just like they had practiced it, all together. Then they begun a new set and it wasn't long before I got caught up in it again. This time they come to a slam-bam finish that had my heart just throbbing. I upped and whooped and clapped again, and still the rest of them zombies just sat there gaping at me. Now there was an excuse for it with Monroe. He was so out of his mind with love that he didn't know what was proper behavior. But these other folks was being down-right rude, it seemed to me. I had to remind myself that I was a guest in the house, and I sat back down and shut up. But I didn't like it.

The next time the musicians come to an end — and it was just a stirring end too, with the music so grave and melancholy — I just sat there on my hands, biting my lips, crinkling my toes in my shoes. If this was the Texas way, I would go along.

But then the next time they come to an end, the most rousing yet, didn't the place just explode! Mr. Corbett hollered and stomped and clapped. Mrs. Corbett clapped and said, "Bravo!" Mrs. Landover was on her feet, her eyes just streaming tears, her hands going sixty. Even Tally and the tom yowled together. Me and Monroe joined in, but it did seem strange.

Ira and Mary and April May stood and bowed, then left the room with us still clapping, which seemed to me rude once again. But pretty soon here they come back again, bowing and curtsying, and the applause swelled. And they left the room again.

Then only Ira come back in. He took his seat at the piano, and we all heshed and settled back to listen. He give us a solo piece, and it was something I'll never forget.

He attacked that piano, him so small and it so grand, like a panther, all stealth and claws and muscle. His eyes snapped and sparked, and the piano cried out under him. I could scarcely believe it was the same Ira-Grub.

The evening was over much too soon, and we bid good-night to the Corbetts and thanked them and climbed back into Mrs. Landover's hack. I stole a look over to Ira to make some sense of what I had seen tonight. He was back now to the same old Ira-Grub, blinky-eyed and little and wan, looking for all the world like he wasn't good for nothing but bait.

Mrs. Landover slapped the reins and the blue roan pony headed off. Ira-Grub shared the seat with her, while me and Monroe and Mary sat in the bed of the wagon on the mattress from the shanty. I thought to myself that it was a mighty peculiar arrangement. If I was the mother, and there was a fellow like Monroe in the back of my hack, I'd sit my daughter right down next to me where I could keep an eye on her. But it seemed that Mrs. Landover had a precious particle of her heart that was owned by Ira-Grub and she just had to have him at her side, and the seat wasn't big enough for Mary, too.

I sat close up behind the seat so I could be as near Mrs. Landover as possible. Monroe and Mary sat further back, him just mooning over her, and her as distant as ever now that April May was left behind.

It got so dark so fast out on that country road with only the light from a little waning crescent moon. The stars seemed like you could reach up and grab a few, but they didn't throw no light to speak of. And the sky was just thick with clouds, the moon dodging first behind one, then another. The pony, though, knowed the way home and stepped along surely, sending back a *clop-clop* sound to accompany the creaking of the hack and the crunch of the wheels.

Presently Mrs. Landover said, "Play us your harmonica, Monroe."

Well, this was a swell idea. I didn't even know Mrs. Landover knowed about Monroe's French harp, but I guess on some of those nights when Monroe tooted a little upon retiring, his eyes on the window of Mary's room, some of the sounds must have drifted over to the big house, and Mrs. Landover heard it then.

Monroe said, "I don't like to, Mrs. Landover, after the fine music your children have played tonight."

Mary smirked, and I had to grip the sides of the hack to keep from reaching over and smacking her.

"Nonsense," Mrs. Landover said. "Play us a tune, Monroe."

It was all Monroe needed. I just imagine he was aching to blow, him sitting right beside his beloved on a darkly star- and moon-lit night, and all that romantic folderol sifting through his blood. He cleared the pipes, then slewed into his favorite, "Red River Valley," and I don't suppose he ever played it better nor more sad, slowing it up and giving it an air you could almost feel a breeze by. Listening to him blow, Mary's smirk melted right off her face.

Going into the second verse, Mrs. Landover begun to sing along with him. Now, I have never known opera, other than the Grand Ole Opry in Nashville, and I know they're not the same. Sometimes today when you're tuning the car radio, you'll hit on some opera, and if you're like me you slide right on past because such a lot of hooting and anguish seems to me bad for the digestion. But this night out on that prairie under that sky, when Mrs. Landover opened her mouth and sung the words to "Red River Valley," I had all I could do to keep from breaking down.

Won't you think of the home you'll be leaving?
Won't you think of how lonely you'll be?
Won't you think of the girl you'll leave grieving?
Won't you think, won't you think, dear, of me?

Mrs. Landover put her arm around Ira-Grub's shoulder and tried to pull him close, but he shrugged, and she took her arm away. I'd have give anything if then she turned to me and offered me her arm. You can bet I'd have melted into it. From the bed of the hack, I yearned up toward her, so close I could smell the cologne in her hair, her soft hair which she was wearing down around her shoulders tonight, dark and curly. But she never turned to me, just moved along into the chorus.

Come and sit by my side if you love me,
Do not hasten to bid me adieu,
Just remember —

She broke off as we become aware of a ruckus behind us. There had been car headlights coming up, getting ever closer ever faster. At first I didn't pay much mind, being intent on the sound of Mrs. Landover's voice. I wasn't worried about being run over because we had us a little lantern hung off the back of the hack. And on this dark a night on this rough a road, most automobiles would be taking it slow and cautious so as not to tear out their bottom on a high center.

But this here car coming now was barreling down on us at such a speed that I thought we was goners. At the last minute, though, it screeched its brakes and skidded to a stop just inches away from us, its lights blinding after so much darkness.

Four men jumped out, wearing white robes and hoods and waving guns. I like to die right there.

Ten

THERE WAS A hullabaloo of voices.

"Who is it?"

"It's the Landovers."

"Is he there?"

"I don't see him."

"Who's that tall one in the back?"

"What color is he?"

"What's your name, boy?" one of them said to Monroe, shoving a gun in his face. It had a long barrel on it and looked awful ugly and mean.

"Don't say a word to them!" Mrs. Landover said quick to Monroe. "These men are scum. Don't talk to them."

"We don't want no trouble with you, Mrs. Landover," the man said, turning to her with his gun turning, too. Ira-Grub tried to jump down, but Mrs. Landover grabbed onto him and held him there.

"You think you scare me, Luke Vale? Dressed like a ghost? Afraid to come out in the daylight like a man? You are nothing but a coward. And you others — Jim Armstrong, Ezra Howe, Zeke Howe. You think because you put a hood on your head, I don't know who you are. You're pathetic. I'd know you in hell."

The men shuffled at hearing their names called out, but the one man who seemed to be their leader, the one Mrs. Landover called Luke Vale, he said again, "We're not after you, Mrs. Landover, so —"

"Who are you after?" she said. "Some colored boy? What did he do? Forget to bow to you? Or maybe he didn't say thank you when you kicked him?"

"Let's go, boys," Luke Vale said. "He ain't here."

They got back into their car, reversed a little, then pulled around us. I seen now that it was a big old La Salle they was driving, brand new.

Mrs. Landover got to her feet in the hack, yelling for all she was worth. "I spit on you!" she said, and spit right onto the windshield of that La Salle, a good, healthy gob that the driver couldn't veer from under. Mrs. Landover kept yelling after them as they spun back onto the road: "If God hears me . . . ! If God hears me . . . !" But she didn't finish. She sat back down on the seat of the hack and started sobbing. I wondered if these was the same men who killed her husband. I wondered if she knowed.

We was all quiet for the longest time, when Monroe come up from the back and said, "Get in back, Ira." Ira did as Monroe told him, and Monroe crawled over the seat and took up the reins and clucked to the pony, and we went on along our way.

By and by as we rolled along, Mrs. Landover got control

of herself and straightened her back and took charge of the reins again. She didn't say nothing, and neither did any of us. Monroe crawled back over the seat, and Ira-Grub took his place again beside his mother.

At home, we all said goodnight, none of us talking much above a whisper. It was awful gloomy. Me and Monroe took the mattress out of the hack and carried it back to the shanty. He was acting fidgety, and I knowed something was up. I was taking off Ira-Grub's suit and hanging it up when Monroe said that he had to go out and take a leak. Well, I knowed that one well enough, having used it more than once myself, and so I kept my eye on him through a crack in the door. Generally he just went right outside, but this time he went over to the driveway and leaned up against a fence post to wait. And pretty soon out come Mary to meet him.

Them two. They had arranged a little farewell rendez-vous. I thought about crashing their little party, figuring it was my duty to Marge. But before I could act, I seen Monroe reach over to Mary and get familiar, and she hauled off and give him a slap that like to snap his neck and that echoed all the way inside the shanty. She turned on her heel and strode back to the house, leaving him alone and spitting. I quick jumped into bed so he wouldn't know I had been up watching. And into the shanty he slammed, just raging.

"Get up!" he said. "We're getting out of this rathole!"

I said, "Now?"

He didn't say nothing but throwed me my clothes, changing out of Mr. Landover's good suit of clothes so rough that I feared he'd rip them.

I said, "I can't go without saying good-bye to Mrs. Landover!"

He said, "Then go say it!"

I pulled on my clothes and made up a little packsack for myself. It was pretty substantial, too, what with the change of clothes that Mrs. Landover had give me, and a little drinking cup that Ira-Grub had give me for a keepsake which had a picture of Babe Ruth hitting a home run over the center field fence for the New York Yankees. In my pocket I put the money I had made from Mrs. Landover which amounted to nearly fifteen dollars. It would have been more, but I had bought a parting present for Mrs. Landover, a blue bandanna like the one Marge had give me.

I made sure that the shanty was in order, sweeping it one last time, then took up my packsack, Ira-Grub's suit and Mr. Landover's suit, and headed for the house. The lights was still on, so I made bold to knock on the back door. Mrs. Landover answered it in her nightgown, so it was clear she was going to bed. Her hair had just been brushed and her face washed, and she looked awful sweet and tender after her cry.

"Why, Blue," she said. "What's wrong?"

"I guess we're leaving, Mrs. Landover," I said, "and I come to say good-bye." I handed her the two suits.

"You're not leaving tonight?" she said.

"Yes, ma'am. Monroe says so."

Mrs. Landover cocked an eyebrow at me, and I could see at once she understood just what had happened. She was awful wise.

She said, "How is Monroe?"

"Oh, he's just fine. He says to say good-bye, too. And we thank you very kindly for all the kindnesses that you have shown us."

Now I took out the blue bandanna and handed it to her. I didn't have no wrapping paper for it, but I had picked a posy of marguerite daisies and tied the corner of the bandanna around it, so it looked gifty enough. Mrs. Landover didn't take it at first but just looked at it in my hand. I feared maybe I had offended her, and didn't know how or why. But finally she accepted it, and she smiled.

I looked away and shuffled my feet, fearing I was going to cry. I hadn't felt like this before. When I left Mama in Atoka, I had stole away and hadn't even said good-bye. This here with Mrs. Landover was terrible. It seemed like going off from her, I was leaving a great chunk of myself behind. She leaned forward and took me in her arms just like I ached for her to. I lost my breath.

I didn't allow myself to stay long in her arms, but pulled away, and without saying nothing, cause I couldn't, I went and found Monroe, and we walked off. I looked back a couple of times and seen her standing outside the door with the light falling on her. Then once I looked back and the door was closed and the light was gone. And I didn't look back again no more after that.

I was so mad at Monroe, and him so mad at Mary, that we didn't say nothing for a long spell but just crunched down the road at the fast clip that anger will carry you. We was on the road to Filigree, and if we legged it, we might reach town in time to catch the early freight out. Me and Monroe had already talked it over in the days before, and had decided to keep on going south and hook up with the Southern Pacific Railroad and take it through El Paso and on to Tucson and Phoenix and finally to Los Angeles on the southern route.

As we walked I begun thinking of those tracks, and the more I thought, the more I sloughed off the heaviness in my heart over leaving Mrs. Landover. I could sense Monroe's blues lightening, too. And by and by come a better humor, a look to the future, to the tracks ahead. Travel is a wondrous thing, and that's a fact. It's the quickest way there is of relieving you of the dumps.

After a couple of miles, we come to a little bridge crossing a little crick that babbled up at us. Monroe pulled over to the side of the road, saying, "I got to take a leak."

I said, "Why, Monroe! You just went not a half hour ago! Your kidneys dribbling?"

He said, "Shut up."

I grinned and joined him on the edge of the bridge and we took our leaks together into the crick. It is a curious thing how the sound of running water can be so invitational like that. We was kids and didn't know nothing at all about germs and disease and pollution, and it was just as natural to us as anything to join our water with that crick.

"My!" I said to Monroe, making a king-sized anatomy joke as we stood on the bridge dangling over the crick. "Ain't that water down there cold!"

Monroe laughed, and in a second come back with, "Yeah, not too deep though!"

We both laughed. And I guess we was friends again. We shook ourselves off and started back down the road.

I had been aware for some time of a glow up yonder

from behind a rise. I had thought it was the lights of Filigree, though it did seem to me we wasn't anywhere near town yet. But now when we come around a bend, I seen that it was the headlights of a car shining out over a field. There was some figures out in front of the car doing something, but we was too far away to see.

Just then the sounds of a woman's screams come to us. "Don't! Don't! Don't!" That was all we could make out. But the screams was frantic and horrible to hear.

Me and Monroe started to run, not knowing what we was running into. But when you hear someone scream, you just got to go to them, or what are you worth?

Coming hard down on them, we lost sight of the spot for a second as we dipped into a little depression. Then we come over the rise and we slowed up, going more cautious now. And then we seen what we seen.

There wasn't no sense in hurrying on in. The woman had stopped screaming now but was sitting on the running board of that new La Salle we had met earlier with Mrs. Landover. She wasn't much of a woman at all, really, just a girl maybe as old as sixteen. Her face was red-blotched and swoll up from crying, but otherwise she didn't seem harmed. In the glow coming back from the headlights, her hair looked like thin string, that limp, whitey color. Her eyes was fixed and staring, like the eyes of a turtle I seen once that those mean Boone boys had upturned onto its back in the sand after cutting off its arms and legs.

One of the men from the La Salle was leaning over her, his foot up on the running board beside her. I recognized his voice. It was Luke Vale. He was talking very soft to the girl, with a gentleness in his voice.

"Wanda? Wanda, are you listening to me now, hon?"

The girl didn't say nothing nor didn't move neither, but just sat there staring ahead.

"Wanda, now this had to be done," Luke Vale went on. He sounded, though his voice was much deeper of course, the way Miss Hudson at school did one day when a little girl in primer had lost her dolly down the well. "You got to marry a boy of your color, honey. There's John Anderson. You know the way he feels about you. Or how about that nice Andy what's-his-name? Don't you like him, honey?"

The girl didn't say nothing for a second, then she said, "Yes." And she catched a sob and sniffled a little.

"Well then? You see? You'll forget this. You'll thank me, honey, you will. If you had married that boy there and bore his children, little brown children, do you think there's a person would even say hello to you? His people wouldn't want you either, honey. You keep from them Mexicans, Wanda. You're a white girl.

"And think of the children. Do you think it would be right for the children? Do you? You always must think of the children. Do what's right for the children. Hmmm?" He give her a moment, then said again, "Hmmm?"

"Yes, sir," she mumbled.

"So tomorrow afternoon," he said, putting his arm around her waist and helping her off the running board, "I'll come over to see your daddy, and I'll bring Andy with me. Would you like that?"

"Yes, sir."

I'll never forget any of what he said. His words and voice are burned into my brain because of what I was watching all the time I was hearing him talk. The three other men was out in front of the car, the headlights showing up every detail of what they was doing. They had taken off their robes and hoods and was hard at work with long knives, very serious, not making a sound or extra movement. They was like those butchers in the slaughterhouse in Filigree that first day we come into town, quiet and professional.

I couldn't see anything about the boy they was working on but that he didn't have on any clothes and that his skin was brown. In the white light of the headlights it hadn't even a touch of gold to it but was just flat, flat brown. His hair, though. It's what I keep coming back to all these years later. His hair must have been his pride. It was so black and thick and wavy, and shiny in those headlights, just radiating a black light of its own. Even with what they was doing to the rest of his body, even when they grabbed hanks of his hair as a handhold to turn him over or pull him into better light, when they let it go again, his hair fell back into place just so beautiful.

The rest of him I can't tell you about. Every feature of his face, they carved off. The parts of his body they hated, they carved off. I prayed to myself that they had killed him first, before they started.

You kids, of course, have growed up knowing about atrocities like this. What the Germans did to the Jews in World War II, what the Japanese did to their prisoners, what the Iranians did just a few years ago to the bodies of those dead helicopter pilots. These is pictures they show now on the TV. There isn't a kid alive in America who

126

doesn't know everything there is to know about atrocity.

But I was a kid before TV. I didn't know. Hadn't no idea. That a human being could be so cruel, so worse than an animal, so evil. Once you have that knowledge, you can never again not have it. And you grow up awful fast.

This country would have you believe it could never happen here, that those other peoples is monsters, but not us. Don't you ever believe it. Men as brutal as the worst of them is all around you in this country. Put a knife in their hands and give them a gang to hide in, and they're set to do their worst. All you can do is pray that you're better than that, that you'll never be one of them.

So here's Luke Vale talking so kind to that poor girl, salving her, helping her up off the running board and getting her back on her feet. That's when he turns, Luke does, and he sees me and Monroe. We've pulled in too close, and we're showing up in the halo of the headlights. Luke stops dead in his tracks, looking us right in the eye. The girl ain't seeing nothing, though she's looking right at us, too.

Luke takes a second, then says, "Men?"

The butchers all stop and look over their shoulders, and then they see us, too. One of them still has aholt of the boy's head, and as he turns, his hand turns too, and the boy's head turns, just like he's looking at us, too. Only there ain't nothing left in his face to look with.

All of them stand silent for a long minute, gauging us, it seems. Then the one who has aholt of the boy's head holds out his other hand to us. In it he's got a long, thin, boning knife. He grins, inviting me and Monroe to join in.

It's like me and Monroe has one mind. We turns together and we runs. First we hear shouts behind us, then
gunshots. But we're gone into the dark, hitting that road
for all we're worth. I hears bullets screaming alongside
my head, but they just gives me more speed.

At first we sticks to the road. But pretty soon from behind us we hears the roar of the La Salle as she starts up
and comes after us. She swings onto the road, and her
headlights picks us up and throws our shadows ahead of
us, great, long, leaping shadows. And we sees at once we
gots to get off the road or she'll run us down.

It's pasture land off to our right and a field of sorghum
off to our left, both with barb wire fences setting them
off the road. We chooses the sorghum field and breaks
away to the left. Monroe jumps over and I bellies under
the wires so quick that our stride is hardly broke.

It's not to our good luck the way this field of sorghum
is laid out, the rows running perpendicular to the road.
Running uphill in the lane between the rows, though we
makes good time, we also makes good targets.

The La Salle comes squealing to a stop behind us,
slewing around so her headlights is shining up the lane
after us, lighting us up like two spare pins in a bowling
alley. Gunshots start ringing out again, and I hears the
bullets slap the dirt and the canes all around us. This
sorghum is about four to five foot high and beginning to
head up, and it makes walls on either side of us that seem
to reflect the light between them and to brighten it. Monroe pretty easy jumps the row of sorghum to the right and
gets into the next lane, and then jumps over that row into

the next lane, and then over that into the next lane, and the next, and the next, until he's moved over several lanes and out of the headlights' beam.

My legs is too short to make the jump, so I just pushes through the canes, row after row chasing after Monroe. The edges of the leaves is sharp and slicey, and I gets plenty cut up dodging through that sorghum, but I finally pulls out of the headlights' beam, too.

Behind us, we hears the yells of the men as they jump out of the La Salle and climb through the barb wire to chase us on foot. Then the La Salle maneuvers again and lines herself up with the new lane me and Monroe is running in, lighting us up again. Again guns start firing at us. We're almost out of range of the headlights now, but ahead of me I sees Monroe's back, and it looks awful broad and easy to hit in the light there is. I pushes over another few rows to the right and Monroe jumps, too. Then comes a gunshot, and it's like it's got Monroe's name on it, like I knows this is the one even before I hears it shot. Down he goes. He's hit.

He's up again in a split second, but he's limping now, and I can see blood spurting out of the inside of his left leg, and it looks like a whole lot of blood. He was hit up high as he was turning to leap the row, and it looks like the bullet cut an artery. Still he can run, and he does, pushing through the rows of sorghum till he gets over to my lane and we're both out of the headlights again. We keeps running, him faltering now, until we gets well beyond range of the headlights even if the La Salle tries to maneuver again to our new lane.

I gains on Monroe and I sees that he's in pretty bad shape. The flow of blood isn't lessening. He don't look like he's going to last much longer. Meanwhile, behind us, I can hear the men coming after us on foot. Looking over my shoulder I sees them clear enough in the headlights, but they can't see us no more because we're out of range, and that little crescent moon ain't bright enough to show us up. We gots a good start on them. And now they're slowing down, starting to fan out, each taking a couple of rows to search, shouting to each other.

"Can you see them?"

"I think they're in your lane, Ezra. Keep a sharp eye."

"No, I think they went on over to your right, Jim."

"Turn off the lights! Turn off the damn headlights!"

That Ezra is in our lane all right, cause we're still traveling in the same path, trying to get as much of a lead on them as we can. But Monroe is staggering now, and I can see that pretty soon he's going to drop. If we don't get out of this lane, all Ezra has to do is keep on coming, and we'll be right there in front of him, sitting ducks.

"Monroe!" I whispers. "Follow me." And I slips through the row to our left, and then again and again. Any other time, I would follow Monroe, and he knows I knows it. But now, he ain't in no condition to lead, and we both knows that, too.

As quiet as we can, we slips through row after row of sorghum, always going to the left. The men behind us is still spreading out to the right, looking for us. It shows you just how stupid a man can be, to figure that just because we started changing rows to the right, that that's the way we're going to keep changing rows.

130

The La Salle has turned off her lights now, so I can't see the men anymore. But they're still making a deal of racket, so it's easy enough to hear that we're gradually leaving them behind. I even starts thinking to myself that if Monroe can keep going, we might get out of this yet. But then, just like bringing on your own bad luck by thinking about it, Monroe falls to the ground.

"I can't go on, Blue!" he whispers.

And from the men, I hears Luke Vale's voice.

"Hesh, you men! Hesh!"

"You hear something?" "Hesh!"

Monroe lays panting at my feet, and I turns and looks off toward where I knows the men is standing, lost in the darkness off yonder. In the moonlight I can see maybe twenty to thirty feet, no more. The men is a good distance beyond that. But that little moon is heading down to the horizon now, and damn if it don't seem to get bigger and brighter as it goes down. The clouds that was chasing around it earlier seem to have chased off, and that sky looks awful clear up there.

I thinks fast. This sorghum is good and thick, and it's got a lot of weeds growing up among the rows. It's possible me and Monroe can simply hide out, laying ourselves up along the base of the sorghum, covering ourselves with the leaves and weeds. In the dark the men might walk right past us.

But Luke is thinking fast, too. "We got to go about this methodical, men," he says, his voice coming across the sorghum out of the darkness. "I hit the big one, I'm sure of it. There's some blood here on these leaves, and it looks like a good hit. He's not going far. Now, they're probably already laying up in one of these rows. Sing out where you're standing."

"Ezra here."

"Zeke here."

"Jim here."

"Okay," Luke says. "We're each going to take a lane. Pull yourself up a stalk and strip off the leaves to make a good, sturdy cane. Thrash upside the base of the plants as you go. We'll drive them out.

"And keep quiet," he says. "If they try to move, we'll hear them. And in any case, I figure daylight's not much more than an hour off."

This is the worst of it. I don't have any idea how big this sorghum patch is, but I do know that if we try staying on where we're laying now, it's only a matter of time until they finds us. When that sun starts to come up, we're done for. There's only one thing for us. We gots to get out of this sorghum patch while it's still dark.

"Monroe," I whispers, "you gots to walk. Can you?"

"Yeah, I think so. But I don't know how far. And I'll be making a lot of noise, Blue. You go on without me."

"You out of your mind?" I says. "Listen to me, now. You think you can make it back to that bridge where we took a leak?"

"I think so. But it'll take me a while. I'm feeling pretty weak."

"Okay. You go there. And you hide out under it. I'll meet you there when I give these guys the shake. I'll bring help. You wait for me now, you hear? I may get hung up, but I'll be there. You hear?"

"Yeah. Okay."

"Now I'm going to get you plenty of room. They won't hear you. See you at the bridge."

"What are you going to do?" he says, starting in to argue.

"Don't you worry," I says, and pushes off quietlike through the sorghum, heading right towards the men.

"Blue . . . !" I hears him start to say, but I don't hang around to hear any more. I gots my plan now, and I'm not going to let Monroe get in the way of it.

There's a lot of quail around Atoka, and these quail is pretty smart little game birds, and there's a trick I learned off them. If a hen quail has got a nest in the grass, and a hound or a fox comes around too close to that nest, this hen shuts up her chicks and comes flopping off her nest, and fumbling and fluttering around and making a big racket. The fox thinks she's hurt, and so he goes after her. Every time he gets close and makes a grab for her, she takes to the air, not far enough to get all the way away, but just enough to keep out of the fox's jaws, yet still keep him interested and chasing after. And she keeps flopping along, leading him further and further from her nest. When she's sure the nest is safe, she just takes to the air, thumbing her nose at that dumb fox, and she circles on back to her chicks.

So that's me now. First off, I takes me a fix on the North Star. In this darkness, it would be easy to lose my bearings and maybe lead those guys slap into Monroe. Then I creeps towards the men as quiet as I can, guiding myself by their noise. They're still making a healthy racket, beating the bushes for me and Monroe, so I'm able to pull up pretty close without them hearing me. It's hard to know just how close I dare. They sound like they're almost on top of me, but still I can't see them.

First I starts up a whispering. It's all gibberish, but I makes it sound like a scared kid about to be found, something like, "I'm getting out of here! I'm running!" Something like that.

"Listen!" one of the men says.

That's when I runs. I heads towards that North Star and I makes as much noise as I can, thrashing the sorghum and whispering and calling, "Look out!" and suchlike, running top speed.

It works. Behind me I hears the men yell and come crashing along after me. A few gunshots ring out, but I'm running low to the ground, and they don't come anywhere near me.

"Here they are!"

"Over there!"

"Over here! Over here!"

I gots all the advantage now. All of us is running blind, but I'm running away; they're running after. And being smaller, I can push a lot easier through the canes. So I leaves them behind real fast, and pretty soon, I hears them slow up again, at a loss. And then they goes back to beating the bushes again.

"Anyone see them?"

"No, but I heard them right next to me. The one sounded lame. They're around here close."

"Watch sharp, now!"

I'm squatting in the lane listening to them, as they move around. And by and by I hears that they've lost me. They're moving further away again, moving back toward where I left Monroe. These are the dumbest men! I sees I gots to go to work again, get them chasing me.

I starts crawling back towards them, once again pulling in as close to them as I dares. A few thinnish, veilish clouds scud over the moon, dimming it a moment before they scud off again. It looks like a bigger cloud is on the way. I decides to wait for it before I makes my move again. If it darkens the moon, it gives me all the better chance of getting away.

As I waits, though, looming up out of the dark just only a few feet away from me now, comes a shadow darker than the rest. It's Luke Vale, creeping along very quiet in the very same lane I'm standing in. He's smarter than the rest of the men, quieter, and he's come along much further than them. He don't see me yet. His head is turning back and forth, his eyes down scanning the base of the plants. He's got a cane in one hand and a gun in the other.

Slowly I sinks in my tracks, into a crouch. I gives a glance up to the moon. The cloud is sliding on in, thickening up, wiping over it. I looks back to Luke. The features of his face is dimming, even as step by step he moves in on me.

And now, just at the moment the cloud blots out the rest of the moon, Luke spies me. His eyes get big, and I see his hand come up and the cane drop out of it as he reaches for me. And now it's black. I springs up from my crouch, and Luke's fingers catches up in the collar of my shirt. I feels the gun bang up against my neck, and I twists and knocks it out of his hand. I twists back and kicks and pulls loose from his grip, but my feet gets tangled up and I falls into the dirt. Luke grabs me again, standing over me between the rows of sorghum and pulling me up. I kicks up at him and some of my kicks hit home, because I hears him grunt.

"There they are!" one of the men shouts.

"Up ahead!"

And I hears a couple of gunshots, and Luke grunts again and falls to his knee. His hold on me loosens. I kicks one last time and breaks free, gaining my feet and taking off like a rabbit with more gunshots ringing out behind me.

"Dammit! Stop them guns, you idiots!" Luke yells. "You hit me!"

I can't keep from laughing. I just hoots as I scours up that lane away from them bastards.

This time I don't stop, but I make real distance before I slows down. I can hear the men still coming after me, but they're way back there now, and I figures they're far enough from Monroe that he can get safe out of the field, too. So I starts making my own way out. That cloud up above is big and dense, and it don't go away. But it don't reach down to the horizon where the North Star is still leading me on. In the blackness, I holds out my hands to guide by the leaves of sorghum on either side of the lane as I hie along.

At last I comes to the end of the row. The sorghum gives out on either side of me. Now I gots to be careful. I can't see nothing at all. I pulls up a stalk and strips it, sweeping it ahead of me like a blind man's cane as I creeps ahead. It hits up against a fence post, and I reaches out with my hand and touches a barb wire fence, dividing the sorghum field from the next piece of property. I climbs through.

The ground on the other side hasn't been plowed. It's hard and dry, a pasture growed over with grass. I keeps the cane sweeping along in arcs ahead of me, and I keeps walking, following after that North Star, putting as much distance as I can between me and them men before sunup.

Eleven

THE WAY MORNING GATHERS itself together is a soft, wonderful thing to be a part of. And it ain't nowhere more glorious than out in the middle of a dark and lonely pasture.

At first I wasn't sure. The light started off in the east, so faint in the blackness that I couldn't really say it was light at all. Then I become aware that yes, I could see. Not much. Not far. But it wasn't any longer all purest blackness. There was the ground under my feet. A few feet ahead, there was a clod. I would have stumbled over that clod a few seconds ago, but now I could see it and walk around it.

And when I looked to the eastern sky again, I could definitely see a light now, even a color, a reddish, pinkish color in the clouds there. The light reflected dimly down to the earth, and I could make out a horizon. I turned, following the horizon around, and the line faded into black behind me. I turned back and kept walking.

In a few minutes, I was able to see all around me good and clear. I was very happy with where I was. There wasn't a building nor a road nor a human being in sight. I was out in the middle of a big, empty range, and I had left the sorghum field way behind. I had come over many little rises and depressions and now I stood alone, with no one near to see me or shoot at me.

I turned eastward, figuring that was where Mrs. Landover's farm would lay. I would go to her and tell her what had happened. Then together we'd take her hack to pick up Monroe at the bridge. He'd need a doctor to look after his bullet wound. And while he was getting fixed up, me and Mrs. Landover would go for the Sheriff to tell him about the murder.

By and by I come to a road crossing my path. I didn't recognize it. This whole countryside was crisscrossed by dirt roads such as this. I thought about taking it wherever it might lead, but decided against it. I'd best stay off the roads in case that La Salle was cruising around looking for me. So I crossed over quick and went on into the next pasture. I kept the rising sun ahead of me, figuring if I went east far enough I'd have to run into or near Mrs. Landover's farm. After a bit, I come upon another road. And now I knowed where I was. The cotton field up ahead was Sam Bellman's land, and beyond it was his corn patch, and on the other side of that was where Mrs. Landover's property started up.

I quick crossed the road and moved along into the rows of cotton. Pretty soon behind me I heard the hum of a motor. I stopped and crouched down. The cotton was only about a foot high, but it hadn't been chopped yet and the plowing was irregular, so there was taller weeds growing up around it. I kept my head up even with the top of the field, waiting as the motor grew louder, getting closer. Then I seen it. It was the La Salle all right, coming slow down the road, with a couple of the men and the white-headed girl Wanda inside, the men's heads slewing this way and that as they watched out the windows for me, looking down the rows of cotton.

I hunkered further down, drawing the leaves up around my head, cursing Sam Bellman for not being able to grow a better stand of cotton than this scraggly, see-through bunch.

But the La Salle kept cruising. They didn't see me. I waited until she was long past and I couldn't hear the sound of her engine no more, then I hightailed it for the corn patch ahead. It was a good healthy stand, almost as tall as I was, with the tops forming up heads of grain. Once I was into the patch, no one could see me moving along, making my way through it.

When I got to the other side, I peeked out through the stalks. In the distance I could see Mrs. Landover's driveway and house. The La Salle was parked right in front. On the veranda stood the two men, talking to Mrs. Landover. Wanda was still in the car.

I held where I was. The morning air always seems thinner to me, and through it now come the murmur of their voices, but they was too far away to catch what they was saying. After a few minutes, Mrs. Landover went into the house, closing the door behind her, and the men got back into the La Salle and drove away. Again they drove slow, their heads turning all about, looking over the countryside. I faded deeper into the corn patch and waited until the hum of the motor died away.

Then I ran out and across the road and up the driveway and leapt the stairs of the veranda two at a time. The door was locked. I pounded on it, calling in a whisper Mrs. Landover's name. She opened the door, and I rushed inside, slamming and locking it behind me. The look on her face was paralyzing, but not so paralyzing as the words out of her mouth.

"Do you want to get us killed?" she cried.

I didn't know what to say at first. I had come to her for help.

I said, "They shot Monroe!"

She said, "You've got to get out of here! They'll come back! You've got to go!"

I said again, "They shot Monroe!"

She screamed at me, "I said get out of here!"

Her voice had a note in it like I'd never heard from her before. I remembered a boy I seen in Atoka who got lost in one of the coal mines. The miners made a search for him, and when they finally found him and pulled him out, he kept screaming, all on this one high note, a crazy sound, the sound of panic. I never expected to hear panic from Mrs. Landover.

"Mrs. Landover!" I said, taking her by the arm and squeezing until my fingernails dug into her skin. "They shot Monroe! They shot Monroe!"

Her eyes was wild. But as I held onto her arm, repeating over and over the only one thing I could think to say, gradually a light of understanding begun in them.

Finally she said, "Where is he? Is he alive?"

"He was," I said. "He's down under that bridge, you know, along on the road to Filigree?" She nodded. I kept

141

talking. "You got to help. We got to get him to a doctor. Then we got to go for the Sheriff. Those men last night killed a man, and . . ."

Mrs. Landover shook her head. "You don't know what you're talking about, do you?"

"Yes! I do! Those men who was just here . . ."

"Those men told me that you killed that Mexican boy! You and Monroe!"

I just stopped, staring at her. Behind her, hiding on the stairway I could see Ira-Grub and Mary, huddling against the wall, their eyes wide and buggy.

"But . . . but . . ." I said, not knowing what to make of anything anymore. "But you don't think that!"

"Of course I don't!" she said. "I know what happened out there. But you don't know these men, Blue. You don't know this town. If those men say you did it, then you did it. They'll hang you."

"But . . . there's the girl. She'll tell."

"Wanda Llewellyn is anyone's dog who'll pet her. She'll tell just what they want her to tell." Mrs. Landover looked at me a long minute, then said softly, "They said that he was . . . mutilated. Did you see him, Blue?"

"Yes, ma'am," I said. I couldn't look her in the eye.

She put her hand out to me and cupped it around the nape of my neck, pulling me to her for a moment. Then she pushed me away and said, "Blue, you've got to get out of this town."

"But I don't know about Monroe. I don't know if he can travel."

Strands of hair had fallen across Mrs. Landover's eyes,

and now she pushed them back, throwing back her head and looking to the ceiling, beginning to think. She was still in her nightdress. Absentlike, she pulled out a couple of hairpins, swirled the hair up and piled it on her head, then pinned it there in place.

"Quick, Blue," she said. "You run out and hitch up the hack. Mary, Ira, go out to the garden and pick the ripest of the melons. Bring them to the barn."

Ira-Grub said, "But they ain't near ripe."

She said, "Do as I say."

I ran out to the barn and got out the hack and the harness and the blue roan pony. Before I was done, Mrs. Landover was working by my side, changed into her riding clothes. "Help me," she said, grabbing up armfuls of hay and tossing them into the bed of the hack. In a couple of minutes, we got it good and full. Meanwhile Mary and Ira-Grub come up with about a dozen watermelons, and Mrs. Landover put them into the hack nestled in the hay, the way you do when you're taking them to market.

"Ira," she said, "you show Blue the secret place." Ira started in to fuss. "Do as I say!" she said. "Take him there and stay with him until I get back. Mary, if anyone comes while I'm gone, you tell them that I've gone to market."

Ira-Grub said, "They're going to think you're crazy, hauling green melons to market."

"They already think I'm crazy," Mrs. Landover said. Then she added under her breath, "Maybe I am."

I said to her, "I'm going with you."

She turned on me, sharp. "Do you know what they'll do to me if they find you with me? You saw that Mexican boy! Do you want me to end up mutilated? Ira, take him!"

Mrs. Landover climbed into the hack, whipped the reins on the back of the pony and pulled out at a fast pace, skidding out of the driveway with the gravel spattering. I didn't give much hope for them watermelons if she kept driving like that.

I turned and followed Ira into the house and down to the cellar. I had been down here before because this is where Mrs. Landover kept her pickling barrels. But now Ira headed way back past the barrels and the other things stored down here, straight to the back wall. There, where you'd never guess there was anything but the wood wall, Ira pulled a lever and slid the wall open. Behind it was a little room about ten by ten, a second, hidden cellar dug out from under the house's veranda. We went inside, and Ira slid the wall closed behind us.

"My Mama dug it," Ira said, "after they shot my Daddy. It was in case they was to come back." He pulled a string, and a low-power light globe come on. Looking proudly over his shoulder at me, he slipped a gun out of its holster where it hung on the wall, and he added, "I guess they're coming back."

There was two little pallets on either side of the dirt floor, and I sank down onto one of them to wait. The long night was beginning to make itself felt. I was awful tired. And my emotions was raw, with the way Mrs. Landover had turned on me. And I was fretting about Monroe. Did he get away or not? How bad was he hurt?

Ira sat on the pallet opposite me, fingering the barrel of his gun and watching me the way a dog watches an empty bowl. He said, "Did you kill that Mexican boy? Really?"

I said, "No."

"Too bad!" he said. "A Mexican would as soon stab you in the back as steal from you, and he'd sooner steal from you than look at you. If you killed a Mexican, good for you."

All I wanted to do was close my eyes and sleep. I had seen too much and heard too much. Always before I could ignore talk like Ira's, stupid people talking big without a thought in their heads about the truth behind their blather. But with that Mexican boy laying out in that field, and the image swirling around in my head of his bloody face and body, and his beautiful hair, I couldn't abide it now.

"You say one more word, Ira," I said to him, "and I'll kick you to hell and gone."

He swelled up and sulked, caressing the gun in his hand in a way that made me want to not close my eyes after all.

The minutes dragged by. I begun to wonder what Mrs. Landover was up to with her watermelons and hay. Was she going for Monroe? Would she find him? Did Monroe make it to the bridge before the dawn? Would she bring him back here? Is that what the hay was for, to cover him up? What if the La Salle come across her? What if the men searched under the hay? What would they do to Monroe? What would they do to Mrs. Landover? Would they come then for me?

These was the thoughts circling in my head as I dropped off into a twitchy kind of sleep. It wasn't a sleep at all. Leastways there was no rest in it. Some time later I woke to the familiar creaking of the hack as it pulled fast into the driveway. Mrs. Landover's voice called out, "Blue, come out here and help!"

I left Ira-Grub sitting on his pallet, slid open the wall, and raced up the cellar stairs and through the house out into the driveway. Mrs. Landover was already pulling Monroe out of the bed of the hack, where he was laying covered over by the hay. All around him laid the watermelons, about all of them busted open. It must have been one hell of a ride.

Monroe was still alive, but it looked like only just barely. He couldn't hold up his head. Some time since I had left him, he had taken off his shirt and tied it as a tourniquet high on his thigh above the bullet wound. His pants and shirt was soaked with blood, and his chest and face was ghastly white.

Mary had come out, too, and was standing at the edge of the hack, gripping the railings, looking down at the blood and Monroe's pale body, frozen and almost as pale herself. I pushed her out of the way, putting myself under one of Monroe's arms while Mrs. Landover got under the other. We worked to get him through the house to the kitchen, sitting him on the edge of the table. He laid back, twisting his head from side to side, moaning and muttering gibberish.

"Go unhitch the hack," Mrs. Landover said to me. "Spread the hay back around the barn and carry the melons out to the pigs. If there's any blood in the hack, clean it up first. Make it look like it hasn't been used. Ira, you go with him and rub down the pony. I don't want him to look like he's been running. Mary, go out to the road and keep watch. If you see anyone coming, you give a call. But don't let it look like you're on watch. Play a game. Play hopscotch. Blue, as soon as you get through out there, come back in here; I'll need you."

All the while she was giving out orders, she was busy setting a fire in the stove and filling up kettles with water. I ran out and unhitched the hack and cleaned it up good, like she said. There was a deal of blood all over, but it come off with some damp rags.

As I was finishing up, I looked out to the road and saw Mary there. She had drawn herself a hopscotch in the dust, and was trying to play, but she kept stopping and looking back at the house. I yelled at her to keep her mind on what she was doing, then ran back to the kitchen.

Mrs. Landover had stripped off Monroe's pants and he was laying stark naked on his back on the table. She had torn some sheets into rags and was sponging his body clean. His skin looked whiter than ever.

"Don't let Mary see," he kept saying over and over, wrenching his head from side to side.

"Run down to the cellar, Blue," Mrs. Landover said as I come in. "There's a jug of corn whiskey on a shelf under the stairs. Bring it up here."

I did as she told me. The smell of the whiskey was ripe, and I judged it had been a home brew of Mr. Landover's cooked up in an illegal still sometime during Prohibition.

"You give it to him," Mrs. Landover said, still cleaning on Monroe. "As much as you can get down him. We've got to cut that bullet out of him."

It wasn't easy to get the liquor into Monroe. He wouldn't swallow, so it dribbled out the sides of his

147

mouth. At length, though, I must've gotten some of it down because he seemed to revive a bit, and a little color come back into his face. His eyes opened and he looked at me and recognized me.

"Blue!" he said. "Tell Mama I'm coming home. I'm bringing a ham."

"Take a big swig," I told him and poured his mouth full of whiskey. He choked on it, but got a lot of it down.

He said, "Tell Marge . . . Tell Marge . . ." His voice was fuzzy and his speech was thick. He was getting drunk all right. "Where's Mary?" he said suddenly.

"Here I am, Monroe," Mary said, coming forward from where she had been standing in the doorway. She was trembling.

Mrs. Landover turned on her. "Get back out to the road!" she screamed. "Do as I told you!"

Mary backed out of the room, looking back at Monroe's body on the table. Mrs. Landover took a skillet from where it was hanging on the wall and slung it at the doorway. Mary screamed and ducked out the door. Through the window I could see her run back out to the road and start up her hopscotch again.

Meanwhile Ira come in through the back door, leaning up against the doorjamb and watching Monroe, his eyes bulging and pale.

"Go out with your sister," Mrs. Landover said to him. "Keep a lookout with her."

"Boys don't play hopscotch," Ira said.

"Do as I say!" she snapped. And Ira slammed out of the house and went out to the road.

Meanwhile I was getting Monroe good and drunk. Mrs. Landover was almost ready, too. She had her knives and a pair of tongs in a kettle of water she had brought to the boil. She took them out now and laid them handy. Then she got a rope and lashed Monroe down to the table, running the rope over across his shoulders and chest and hips while I took another length of rope and tied his legs down good across the thighs and knees and ankles.

Monroe giggled the whole time.

"Eleonora!" he said. "Eleonora! Beautiful Eleonora!"

I was humiliated for him because his body started getting amorous. You'd think that half dead, he'd be beyond it, but that was just exactly like Monroe. Mrs. Landover didn't pay him any attention, though. She was examining the wound, pushing and feeling tenderly around about the bullethole. It was high up on the inside of his thigh, a small-enough-looking hole.

Mrs. Landover said, "It looks as if the bullet hit an artery, he's lost so much blood. There's a lot of dirt in the wound, too. An infection has probably set in."

She went to the counter, pulled open a drawer, took out a wood spoon, and held it up before Monroe's eyes.

"Monroe," she said, "we're going to cut into you now. You chew on this spoon. Yell all you want to."

She slipped the spoon between his teeth, and while Monroe was still giggling, she picked up a boning knife and dug into the wound. Monroe's body jerked stiff as he screamed and strained up against the ropes. He bit clean through the wood spoon.

"He's got the jaws of a bear!" Mrs. Landover said.

149

"Blue, go fish in that drawer. There's a good, sturdy wood spatula in there. Put it in his mouth, and talk into his ear."

I did like she told me, and while she kept digging at him, I put my mouth right against his ear and whispered to him. I don't know what I said, the kind of thing I guess you say into a horse's ear when you're running a race, stroking his neck, saying a lot of nothing. And the whole time he kept thrashing on that table.

Finally Mrs. Landover cut down to the bullet. She picked up the tongs and slipped the arms into the wound and gripped the bullet and hauled it out. Monroe fainted dead away.

Just then we heard a yell from Mary.

"Mama! The Sheriff's coming down the road!"

Mrs. Landover yelled back to her. "Stop him out there, Mary! Keep him talking!"

We cut the ropes off Monroe and together we drug him off the table and down the stairs into the cellar. He was bleeding again, and Mrs. Landover stopped long enough to take off her apron and tie up the wound with it. Then we drug him across the cellar, slid open the wall to the secret room, and heaved him inside onto the pallet.

"You clean up those tracks," Mrs. Landover said to me. "I'll try to keep the Sheriff away from you."

She went back up the stairs, tossed me down Monroe's clothes and the bloody rags, then closed and locked the cellar door. I throwed the rags into the hidden room. Then I took off my shirt and swept the dirt floor with it, trying to wipe out where we had drug Monroe across it. But if you looked close, you could still see the tracks plain enough, leading straight to the false wall. I tried to disguise the tracks by moving the barrels around, but then you could see that the barrels had been moved. Everything I did to cover it up seemed to make it all the more obvious.

Overhead, I could hear Mrs. Landover banging around the kitchen, trying to get the table cleaned up. Faintly in the distance I could hear Mary out in the driveway talking a mile a minute at the Sheriff. I couldn't tell what she was saying to him, but she was managing to hold him off, all right.

Finally, though, I heard the clump of his boots climbing the stairs up to the veranda and a knock on the front door. I heard a couple of last sounds from Mrs. Landover above me in the kitchen, then her footsteps as she went to answer the door. I looked around the cellar. I had done what I could. Maybe if the Sheriff come down here, maybe if he didn't turn on the light, maybe he wouldn't notice the tracks. I slipped into the secret room and slid the door shut behind me, flicking off the little light globe. I slipped the gun out of the holster hanging on the wall, and crept over and sat down on the pallet next to Monroe. He was starting in to shiver, naked in the cold of the cellar. There wasn't anything to cover him up with but the bloody rags, so I curled my own body around him, and for a moment he seemed to stop trembling so much.

Through the planking of the veranda above me, I could hear the voices of the Sheriff and Mrs. Landover just as though they was in the room with me.

"Morning, Mrs. Landover."

"Morning, Sheriff."

"You heard, I guess, about them boys of yours."

"They're not my boys, Sheriff! Zeke and Ezra Howe came by here this morning and told me those boys are murderers!"

"Well, that's the way it looks. You been harboring some pretty mean fellows. Can you give me their names?"

"I . . ." Mrs. Landover begun, then hesitated. "I don't think I know."

"They didn't tell you their names, Mrs. Landover? How long did they work here? You didn't ask their names?"

"No, of course, I know their first names. But I don't think they ever told me the rest. Monroe was the big one, and the little one was Blue."

"Was they brothers?"

"They said so. But I suppose murderers would be liars, too, wouldn't they, Sheriff?"

"Do you know where they are now?"

"No, they left here last night."

"Did they tell you where they was heading?"

"No. Wait, I remember. I think I overheard the big one saying he wanted to go north. Up into Kansas, I think."

"And you haven't seen them this morning?"

"No! I only pray I never see them again!"

Monroe give a little moan. I clapped my hand over his mouth and held on tight. He was shivering again. But he kept still. In the dark I couldn't tell if he had wakened or not. If so, and if he was in his right head, he would be scared, wondering where we was. But I didn't dare even whisper to him with the Sheriff right above us. I kept my hand over his mouth, and stroked his forehead with the other hand.

"Would you mind if I took a look around?" the Sheriff said. "Not that I don't trust you, Mrs. Landover. I know you want to see justice done as much as anybody. But we got to be on the safe side."

My heart jumped up into my throat. If he come down into the cellar. If he seen the tracks. If Monroe moaned again. I searched out with my hand and found the gun, laying between us. I picked it up and held it tight.

"I wish you *would* look, Sheriff!" Mrs. Landover cried. "I've been so scared ever since Ezra and Zeke told me! Why, those boys mutilated that poor Mexican boy! And they lived right out back! Any night they wanted to, they could have come in here and slit our throats! I'm so afraid they might come back!"

"Oh, well . . ."

"We need protection, Sheriff! Couldn't you post a man here? Couldn't you stay yourself?"

"Now, I wouldn't worry, Mrs. Landover. Those boys would be crazy to come back here."

"There are so many places here to hide! The barn! The storm cellar! Please stay! Couldn't you? For the children's sake!"

"Now, don't start letting your imagination run away with you, Mrs. Landover."

"Please, Sheriff! Come out to the barn with me, now. And that little house back there where they slept? I'm so afraid! Please stay!"

"Mrs. Landover, I got a lot to do today! I can't be hanging around here watching over you! All right, I'll check the barn for you, but that's all! You got to get aholt of yourself now!"

I heard the clump of their feet going down the front steps, and their voices as they faded away with Mrs. Landover still begging at him for protection. I guess that woman had about the coolest, levelest head that I ever seen.

Twelve

THE SHERIFF LEFT without doing much of a search. He never even come into the house. Mrs. Landover seen to that. She pestered him so much for protection that he shied clear off the place as quick as he could go.

When he was gone, Mrs. Landover come down to the cellar, bringing clean clothes with her and some blankets. Monroe was still shivering with the cold, and now a fever had set in.

Mrs. Landover had a needle and thread with her, too. She sewed up the wound in his leg, which was quite a gash now with all the cutting she had done to dig out the bullet. She did a good, proper job, putting in stitches deep inside the wound as well as on the surface. The apron she had tied around his leg earlier had staunched the bleeding, but truth to tell, I don't think Monroe had all that much blood left in him.

After Mrs. Landover got through sewing up the wound, and dressing it, dousing it with iodine, she sat down beside me on the pallet at Monroe's feet, and we watched him together. He was fitful.

After a long time, Mrs. Landover said, "He's lost a lot of blood."

I said, "I know."

"It's a nasty infection."

"I know."

"His tourniquet was very tight. If it was on too long, gangrene will set in. You'll have to cut off that leg. He needs a doctor."

We slipped back into quiet, looking at Monroe. He was in a bad way, moaning and crying out in his fever. Over at the door, Mary stood looking in. Her face was a study, drawn up in worry. For the first time, it seemed to me she looked like her mother. I thought to myself, "You yelpy bitch! You're the one teased him, then chased him away!"

But even as I thought it, I knowed it wasn't fair to Mary. Me and Monroe left here when we left here cause we had to leave. It was time. It was just our bad luck that we happened across that La Salle when we did. It was no fault of Mary's.

"He's making a lot of noise, Mama," Mary said. "I could hear him upstairs."

Mrs. Landover turned to me. "By midday," she said, "they'll have the whole town out looking for you. If they come back by here, you'll have to gag him. Use a pillow to muffle him."

I nodded.

"Then tonight," she said, going on with it, "when it gets dark, I'll take you out and show you where the Old Downey Road runs. It's about a mile from here. No one travels it much anymore. You can take the pony. I'll make up a litter for Monroe. You can get away."

I turned to her and searched her face. I couldn't make out a word of what she was talking about.

I said, "What?"

She said, "You can't stay here, Blue. You have to go."

I said, "Monroe can't move."

She said, "They'll come back. They'll find you. You can't stay here."

I said, "It'll kill him."

She said, "Blue, you have to go! You can't stay here!"

I said, "I can't! It'll kill him!"

She said, "You have to go!"

I took a long minute, looking at her. Then I turned to Mary. Ira come up beside her. All three of them looked back at me in the same way, joined together. They was family.

"I'm sorry, Blue," Mrs. Landover said. "These are my children. I'm not going to risk them for you. Don't ask it."

I couldn't find a word more to say to her. My heart was wrenching.

Through the day, people come by a couple different times. I could hear them through the planking above, asking their questions, trying to involve Mrs. Landover. She was smart about pulling them away from the veranda, to get them out of earshot in case Monroe was to cry out in his fever. I prayed he would keep quiet, and my prayers was answered. He slept heavy and hard.

Once I heard Luke Vale's voice. I had been hoping he was dead, that the bullet wound he got in the sorghum patch had been fatal. But it seems he was just winged. Mama always said, "Only the good die young. The bad, they're charmed."

I slept on and off during the day, but it was a miserable kind of sleep. In my dreams I was running the whole time, fleeing between a pair of warping railroad tracks, the crossties drenched with blood and slick under my feet. Away off in the distance, where the tracks seemed to end, stood a woman. By turns, with the blinking of an eye, she was my Mama then Marge then Mrs. Landover. It seemed like she had something to give me, to help. But the harder I ran, the slower and tireder I got, and the further away she stood, just smiling.

I woke when the sun went down, tireder than if I hadn't slept at all. Mrs. Landover come back down the cellar stairs and stood looking in at me. I couldn't look back.

"You ready?" she said.

I said, "No. But I guess that don't make no difference to you."

I got one arm and Mrs. Landover got the other, and we heaved Monroe up between us. I had dressed him in the clothes Mrs. Landover had brought down that morning, so he was warm enough. But as soon as we moved him, I seen that his pants went red with fresh blood. We must have broke open his wound again, lifting him. Together we drug him up the stairs of the cellar and out the back door. It wasn't easy, and we had to rest a couple of times, but we got him there. Mrs. Landover had the blue roan pony ready. She had built a stretcher for him, the kind I had seen Indians use to haul their belongings, two rails hitched up to the pony's shoulder harness, stretching out behind him as a drag, with ropes tied between the rails as a bed for Monroe. We laid him onto the ropes, and I tied him up under the arms to keep him from sliding off. Mrs. Landover covered him over with a wool blanket.

Mrs. Landover said, "I'd give you the hack, Blue, but the road is too rough. The hack wouldn't make it."

I nodded.

She said, "I put food in the saddlebags for you. There's biscuits and jerky. You have enough for several days. There are extra blankets rolled up there, too, if it turns cold."

I nodded.

"Here," she said, pushing some bills into my hand. "It's all the money I have on the place right now. It's not much, but it will help."

It was nearly twenty dollars. I still had my fifteen dollars in wages, and we had pulled Monroe's money out of his bloody pants pocket before taking them with the rags to burn them. So this made me nearly fifty dollars I was holding in my hand. I might have felt rich, only all I could feel was poor and empty.

Mary come down from the steps to the litter. She pushed the hair back off Monroe's forehead and give him a kiss. Then she come to me and tried to give me a kiss, too, but I pulled away. I couldn't stand the touch of her. Ira wasn't anywhere around when me and Mrs. Landover set out.

We kept to the fields, leading the pony along. We didn't dare take the roads because we knowed the towns-people was still out searching for us. The moon wasn't up yet, but Mrs. Landover knowed the way, and the Milky

Way sliced across the sky throwing off enough light that you could almost cast a shadow by it.

Mrs. Landover didn't say anything, and I didn't say anything back, until we come to an old road. Really, it was hardly even a trail anymore, overgrown with grass and weeds, two wheel tracks stretching off parallel into the distance.

"This is the Old Downey Road," Mrs. Landover said. "You shouldn't meet anyone on it tonight. There aren't many houses between here and Downey, just a few farms off to your right. Downey's about twenty miles away. Maybe they haven't heard about you there. Maybe you can find a doctor."

I nodded.

"If they're looking for you there, too, keep going. There's a railroad in Downey. Going north it hooks up to the Rock Island Line, south to the Southern Pacific. Maybe they won't be guarding the trains so close there. Maybe that's how you can go."

I nodded again.

She said — and here she fell into a little stammer — she said, "Tomorrow I'll report the horse stolen. I guess once they're looking for you for murder, it won't hurt to be a horse thief, too. They can't know I helped you, Blue. If they catch you . . . If they catch you, you'll keep silent about me, won't you?"

I didn't answer right up. She said, "Blue?"

I said, "They won't catch us."

"But if they do, Blue? If they do, what will you tell them?"

"I'll say I stole your horse, Mrs. Landover. I'll keep you safe."

"Thank you," she said. She bent down to kiss me on the cheek, and I let her. I don't suppose ever in my life I hurt.so much as I did at that moment. I took the reins from her hands and started off down the path, leading the pony. I never looked back.

Years later, I run into Ira in San Francisco, and I asked him about his Mama. It was 19 and 55, the year we had so much flooding in California, the year it rained every day for an entire winter. I saw in the newspaper that Ira Landover was in town, giving a piano recital. He was famous, the newspaper said, one of the greatest concert pianists the country had ever produced. There was a picture of him at his piano. I was married to Hannah by this time, and I showed her the picture and asked her if she wanted to drive down to San Francisco to attend. She said no. She said if I was to approach Ira, I'd best do it alone.

Well, I couldn't keep away. I drove down in all that rain, and bought my ticket and stood in line with all those people dressed up in such fine clothes, getting rained on, listening to them talk, the things they said about Ira Landover. Then the doors opened and we went inside, into that beautiful concert hall, and we took our seats. After a long while, Ira come onto the stage, and everyone stood up and clapped their hands at him.

He was the same old Ira-Grub. I'd have knowed him if I'd met him on the street. Pale and shaky walking onto the stage, facing all those people, with his eyes down and inward and skittery. But then when he sat down to the piano, and put his fingers onto the keys, it was like magic. I sat among all those strangers and just wept. And when it was over, you never heard such applause. The people of San Francisco loved Ira Landover.

I went backstage afterwards and waited for him. He didn't notice me at first, almost walked right by me. I had to reach out and grab aholt of his arm. And even then he tried to pull away, thinking I was a fan, I guess.

I said, "Ira, don't you remember?"

Then he looked me in the eye — he had such a pale eye! — and after a moment, he said, "Yes, I remember."

We just looked at each other for a long time. What was there to say, after all?

Finally I said, "How's your Mama?"

He said, "I don't know. I don't see her."

I said, "Is she still in Filigree?"

He said, "No. She went back to Italy. We don't talk."

I said, "What about Mary?"

He said, "She's still there. Got married."

We kicked around a minute or two, but he wanted to get gone, and so did I. We didn't even shake hands or say good-bye. He moved off to his dressing room, and I went on home.

Thirteen

IT WAS A NEVER-ENDING night, that one on the Old Downey Road. It was just me and the pony walking along forever, him in his track, me in mine, the pony's heavy breathing beside my shoulder setting a rhythm for us. The hours walked with us, the stars sweeping slowly by above us. We was heading mostly east, so when the moon rose, it was dead ahead, the crescent slimmer tonight. I watched it through the night climb up the sky in front of us. Then it dropped back behind us, but I wasn't looking back.

Monroe was dead to the world, laying in the litter. I stopped from time to time to check on him. He was still breathing, but it was labored. I figured if I didn't get him to a doctor soon, he wasn't long for the world. It was the only thing kept me going, I guess.

We come to crick after crick. Over some, bridges still stood. But most of them had washed out and wasn't rebuilt. So we just waded across the shallows, dragging the litter through, and kept going. I was dead tired, but my feet seemed to walk on their own. The brain is a remarkable thing, the way you can just stop thinking, just take

163

the next step, the next step, the next step. I didn't know what I would do when I got to Downey. Maybe just keep stepping. Mama always said, "If you don't know what to do next, keep doing what you're doing; it can't be all that bad."

Every once in a while, I reached into the saddlebag and pulled out a biscuit and some jerky. It was good food, good to chew. I wished I could've shared it with Monroe, but he couldn't eat, of course.

Getting around toward dawn, I begun to come in among some houses, and I figured I must be nearing Downey. We come to a railroad track, and I stopped. I looked both ways. It was a tossup. I turned to the right.

After a half mile or so, I seen a jungle up ahead. There was a little stand of trees along a little crick that crossed under the right of way. About a dozen men was laying about in their bedrolls. Only one man was stirring already, and he was up building the fire and filling the coffeepot with water. I wondered if I dared approach him, to find out the news in this part of the country, to find out if they had heard yet about me and Monroe.

While I was still making up my mind, the fellow turned towards me just a hair, and now I recognized him. It was Chicago Stumps. Well, that made up my mind for me. I tied the pony to a tree, and stepped forward.

"Hi, Stumps," I said, coming into the jungle.

He looked up at me like I was a ghost, then quick put his finger to his lips, and come forward and took me by the shoulder and ushered me out of the jungle. When we was several paces away, he whispered to me.

"Where's Monroe?"

I said, "He's hurt," and nodded to where the pony stood.

Stumps walked to him quick and examined Monroe, putting his hand onto his brow.

"He's burning up!" he said.

I said, "Yes. I think he's dying."

Stumps looked at me straight for a long moment, then he said, "Blue, you didn't kill that Mexican boy, did you?"

I said, "No, it was the KKK. They pinned it on us cause we witnessed it."

He said, "I figured it was something like that. The god-damned devils!"

"God damn them!" I said, too, and now for the first time I started crying. As I told you before, only once in my life have I used the Lord's name in this way. And to this day, I still pray that God damned those men to hell.

"You can't stay here," Stumps said, still whispering. "Some of these folks is mean. Even the boes here. You can't trust them. They'll turn you in. Stories have been coming in about you."

I said, "I'm tired. I can't go on. I got no place to go to. Monroe's dying. I want to die, too."

Stumps looked at me for a second, then said, "I know someone who can help. You wait here. I'm coming right back."

He went into the jungle, pulled together his bedroll and packsack, then come back to me and took the reins of the pony.

"Come on," he said.

165

We walked back up the tracks the way I had come, crossed the Old Downey Road, and kept going. I was stumbling from fatigue now, and so was the pony. The ballast crunched under our feet awful loud. I was afraid we would wake the town. Stumps's peg leg made a different kind of sound than his good foot, a kind of screwing sound that give a funny rhythm to his walk.

Pretty soon, we come to the train yard. There was a long freight already made up and ready to pull out. On one of the sidings there was a row of old retired boxcars that the line hands lived in with their families. Stumps drew up the pony there, and leaving me behind, he scouted out the train for a boxcar for us. By and by he come back, hying along as fast as his peg leg could bring him. He waved to me, and I led the pony out from behind the row of retired cars.

We went about halfway back up the train until we come to a boxcar that had been broke into. The hasp didn't close right. Stumps slid the door open, and I could see that the boxcar was only about three quarters full, loaded with cartons marked SHOES and BOOTS. I quick untied Monroe from the litter, and we heaved him up onto the floor of the boxcar. It wasn't easy. I hadn't much strength left, and Monroe was dead weight. Stumps was missing a hand, and though he did make the best use of that stumpy arm of his, we was both sweating by the time we got Monroe half through the door. Stumps climbed into the car after him. Even missing a hand and a foot, he was an agile and strong old guy, and he had developed hisself an easy technique for boarding freights. He got aholt of the belt of Monroe's pants and hauled him the rest of the way in.

"Get rid of that horse," he said to me. I hesitated. He said, "Go! Quick!"

I said, "You got a pencil?"

"What the hell for?" he said, pulling a stub out of his pocket.

I said, "You got to write me a note."

He said, "Aw, hell!"

I said, "Please. It's important to me."

He said, "Okay, okay!" He tore some lining paper off the inside wall of the boxcar and said to me, "Shoot."

I said, "Write this down. 'This horse belongs to Eleonora Landover of Filigree, Texas. I stole it. But now I am sorry and want her to have it back. Please see that she gets it. Reward.'"

I didn't sign my name on it because I couldn't see how that would help. I put the note into the saddlebag and led the pony off the right of way into a good field of grass. I unhitched the litter and set him free. But he didn't know where to go. He tried to follow me when I headed back for the tracks, so I picked up some little rocks and heaved them at him. He shied back away from me, then turned to me again, his eyes too sorrowful to look into. I throwed another little rounded pebble at him, and he turned and trudged off into the field. He was an awful good little horse.

That time with Ira years later backstage at the concert hall in San Francisco, I did ask Ira if the blue roan pony was ever returned. He said no.

I said, "Your Mama loved that pony."

He said, "I know she did."

When I got back to the boxcar, Stumps had already been at work. He had unlashed the load and moved the cartons of shoes around in such a way that he had made a little chamber up toward the head of the car. From the doorway, you couldn't see the chamber. It just looked like a solid load. But there was one carton which could be slid in and out that we could use as an entrance. We laid Monroe out in the chamber, and then I helped Stumps to relash the load to keep it from shifting. We slid the boxcar door closed, then we crawled into the chamber ourselves and slid the carton into place, and we was well hidden.

I had kept one of the saddlebags off the pony, and now I offered Stumps some biscuits and jerky, and I whispered to him the story of what had happened in Filigree. I couldn't make out his face in the darkness, but I could feel him following the story, shaking his head.

When I was finished, he said, "Blue, you mustn't feel bad about that woman. That was a good woman. She did all she could for you."

I didn't say nothing.

"Shhh!" he said. Then we heard the crunch of shoes on the ballast outside our boxcar. Then a shout.

"Hey, Lonnie! Was this hasp broke before?"

There was more crunching. "No sir, I don't believe so!" The boxcar door was slid open. Me and Stumps held our breath. Monroe hadn't made a noise for some time. He was too far gone.

There was a long moment, then the first voice said, "Looks okay." And the door was slid shut again.

"Fix that hasp, would you? And lock up that car again."

My heart jumped. I didn't come this far to be locked into a boxcar and maybe left to die.

"Aw, leave it. Let them take care of it in El Paso."

From away off at the front of the train, I heard that familiar *bump-bump-bump* that meant the train was starting. Pretty soon our car jerked as the couplings engaged, and we was off.

I slept all that day and way into the night. I know we stopped a lot, it being a local, but I just turned over and went right back to sleep. I never was so tired. I never slept so hard. Stumps was watching over us now, and I give him up the job with a whole heart.

Sometime during the night, Stumps woke me and said, "We're here."

I said, "Where?"

He said, "Wellaway."

I said, "What's in Wellaway?"

He said, "A man I know."

We slid out the carton and crawled out, dragging Monroe behind us. He was still alive. We opened the door to the boxcar, and Stumps looked out both ways, then jumped down. With me pushing and him pulling, we got Monroe out of the boxcar and onto Stumps's shoulder. I jumped down beside him, and we made our way off across the right of way.

We didn't go to a jungle, but found a culvert off a ways from the train yard and put Monroe down there. We had come into desert land now, this far south in Texas, real flat, and sandy, and not a thing growing but little thorny scrub plants.

Stumps said, "You stay here with him. I'll be back soon."

And he was gone. I looked at Monroe. It seemed like a long time since I had seen him. He seemed awful far from me. He was looking thin and white and drawn in the moonlight. That same moon shone down on us, that same moon from last night and from the night before, though it had slivered down now to an old moon, almost gone, and though here we was now, so many miles down the tracks. I looked up at it and wondered, how could it be that same moon? How could this be that same Monroe? How could I be that same Blue? I wondered if Mama was watching the moon tonight, too, wondering where her boys was. I wondered if Mrs. Landover was watching it, if Marge Starr was watching it.

Daylight was starting when Stumps come back. He brought a man with him, a black man with a black horse. Both the man and the horse looked worn out with time and work, and neither one looked happy to be drug out of sleep into the night. The man had a sour, wrinkled, frowning face pulled long and clamped shut with a jaw like a beartrap. He stopped when he got to Monroe, bent over him a minute, shaking his head, and then with one movement, and saying nothing, he heaved Monroe up and throwed him across the back of the horse. Then he led off back the way they come. Stumps glanced over his shoulder at me with a look that said, "Shut up and come on."

We kept to the tracks, going further and further out of

town. Then after a while we cut off to the west and come to what looked to be the city dump. We circled it, a whole lot of trash and none too fragrant, and come at length to a little shack built of rusty old sheets of corrugated metal held up by stones and kettles and old wheel rims, or anything out of the dump that had a little weight to it.

There was a girl waiting at the doorway to the shack, a very pretty black girl about Monroe's age. She come forward when we arrived, and as the black man slid Monroe off the horse and carried him into the shack, she followed along the way you might expect a nurse to follow the doctor.

Inside the shack, there wasn't much room, so I stood in the doorway looking in. The man put Monroe onto a mattress which was laying on the dirt floor along one side of the shack, an old, stained mattress with the ticking torn and the stuffing pulling out. He unbuttoned Monroe's pants and pulled them down, the girl pulling on one pants leg and the man pulling on the other. He took a knife and cut away the dressing that Mrs. Landover had bound the wound with. It was matted with dried blood now. He bent over the wound for a minute, examining the stitching, then looked over his shoulder at me.

"Did you do this?" he said.

"No," I said. "A friend."

"Not bad," he said, and looked back at the wound. Then he turned to the girl and said, "Trudy, go bring me some water."

Trudy brushed past me in the doorway, giving me a little self-conscious smile and saying in a soft voice, "Excuse me."

171

I moved back a ways, and she went outside and picked a kettle off the fire. There was a nice little fireplace there built of flagstones, and a couple of different kettles was sitting on the grill with water boiling. She give me that same shy smile on her way back into the shack, setting the kettle down on a little wood platform raised up on flagstones as a kind of table. The man put his hands right down into that kettle with the water still on a boil from the fire. I gasped to see it, but he didn't look like he even felt warm. He rubbed his hands together in the boiling water, then pulled them out and put them hot and steaming on Monroe's wound.

Monroe stirred, pulled stiff, and moaned. The girl took a cloth and dipped it into another kettle of water, this one cool water, and wrung the cloth out over Monroe's forehead. The man kept on at the wound, kneading Monroe's thigh with his hot hands. He muttered under his breath. It sounded like prayers, or like a witch's chant. The girl sung a little song, but I couldn't make out the words. They kept it up for a full hour. Every once in a while he would send her out for more boiling water, and he'd dip his hands in it again. Each time he put his hands back on Monroe's wound, Monroe would cry out, louder and stronger.

One time he yelled, "Blade!"

I froze where I stood. Stumps looked over at me and then to the black man. The black man paused in his work, then went on massaging.

"Blade!" Monroe yelled again, and his voice cracked with pain. "Hold onto my hand! You shouldn't've come at me! I warned you! Hold on! Hold on!" He rolled his

172

head on the mattress. And then come a scream out of him which like to tear out my heart.

"Blade!!!!"

And Monroe fell quiet. The black man kept working for minutes more. Then he stood up away from Monroe, worn out. His back cracked. He was sweating and his black skin looked kindly gray, his eyes yellow-rimmed.

He said, "I gots to sleep."

He stretched hisself out on the mattress next to Monroe, wrapping his long arms around him, and plunging right into a deep sleep. Trudy come up to me and said in that same soft, shy way, "He gots to sleep now."

I backed out of the shack, and she come out with me. She let Stumps out, then pulled the door to.

"Would you care for something to eat?" she said.

"I wouldn't mind," I said.

She fixed up a mess of grits for me and Stumps. He stood there the whole while, looking at me sharp.

"What happened to Blade?" he said.

I held off a second, not knowing if I could trust him. Then I thought of all he done for me and Monroe, and I told him the whole story, what I knowed of it.

"So Monroe killed him," Stumps said at the end.

I trembled. I said, "I didn't want to believe it, but it seems he did."

"But then he give him his hand," Stumps said. "More than I would've done, the fool."

Stumps give me a pat on the shoulder, then took his grits over to sit by Trudy, talking with her in low tones.

I was left alone with my thoughts. They was pretty dreadful. I ran back over that trip on top of the train, me going to sleep, leaving it all up to Monroe. I pictured Blade making the jump across the coupling gap, Monroe shoving the Barlow into him, Blade falling, grabbing on, Monroe reaching for his hand, Blade slipping, then gone. Monroe killed him. And I slept.

I shook myself. I shook myself again until I was clear. "Well," I said to myself at last, "if God don't put Monroe into heaven, then I don't want to go neither."

I looked over to Stumps. He was still talking low to Trudy. I heard him say, "How's Cully doing here? He making it?"

She said, "Oh, he's getting old, Stumps. He's tired."

I remembered in McAlester, Stumps talking about Black Cully, the healer. He told us all that Black Cully was killed by a bull named Rainbow Red. Yet here was Black Cully in Wellaway, Texas. Alive.

Later, when we was washing the dishes, I said to Stumps, "That's Black Cully in there, ain't it?"

He looked at me a second, then said offhandedlike, "Black Cully's dead."

I said, "Yeah, that's what you said in McAlester. Why did you tell that story when that man in there is Black Cully, and he ain't dead at all?"

He washed the same plate two or three times, holding it up to the light, thinking. Finally he said, "Well, Blue, sometimes we get in trouble and it ain't our fault. I guess you know what it's like to be a man on the run, don't you? It'd be good, wouldn't it, if them people in Filigree thought you was dead?"

I nodded.

"So you see, Blue, as far as you know, Black Cully is dead."

"And you're going to keep shut about Blade?" I said.

"What do I got to do with Blade?" he said. "Last I know of Blade, he was in McAlester, alive."

I nodded again.

Then I said, "That girl Trudy, is that Cully's wife or something?"

"That's his granddaughter. His girl's girl."

I said, "She's nice."

He said, "Oh, yeah."

Then I heard Monroe's voice coming from the shack, a kind of bellow. "Hey, Blue!" he said. He sure didn't sound dead.

I ran to the door and pushed it open and the morning light fell on Monroe in a slant. He looked strong. I could have kissed him. He was sitting bolt upright on the mattress looking down with a frown on Black Cully, who was still laying there next to him, snoring.

"Who is this guy?" he said to me.

I said, "You be good to that man! He saved your life!"

Fourteen

MONROE GOT BETTER FAST. Black Cully's hands was a gift from heaven. It was no wonder that Stumps and Whitey and the rest of the boes in McAlester took up for him so quick against Blade. He was an angel on earth.

Years later, Cully did die. I don't know just how. It was Monroe who told me about it, and he made it awful mysterious. He come to visit me out here in California after the war, and that's when he told me about Cully.

That was a surprise, that visit of Monroe's. I hadn't heard from him since he enlisted and got shipped off to the Pacific in 19 and 42. Up until then, he had been living with Trudy, here and there, moving around a lot.

Oh yes, wasn't that just like Monroe! He give up altogether on those Starr girls. Marge, Rose Jewel, Violet Ruby, they become just shadows of a memory next to the luster of Trudy. And Trudy was about as sweet and good as any human being you ever wanted to meet, and she cared the world for Monroe. Why, those first days in Wellaway when she was nursing him from that bullet wound, you couldn't get her away from his side. That's when

Monroe fell in love with her. Well, you know Monroe. Him laying there sick, and a good-looking girl like Trudy watching over him. It wasn't no time before the love sparks was just flying between them.

At first Cully, he tried to discourage them. He didn't want no white boy messing with his granddaughter. But the bonds between beautiful young nurse and handsome young patient could not be rent asunder. Cully may as well have tried to keep the ocean off the shore as to keep Monroe off Trudy. I didn't even try. I had followed Monroe too long, through all the Starr girls, Mary Landover, April May Corbett, and now I knowed him too well. If he wanted Trudy and Trudy wanted him, I was too tired. I said, "Go, Monroe."

And they made each other good and happy for many years. They couldn't get married, of course, leastways not in the South because of him being white and her being colored. It was against the law back then. Ain't it just crazy, the laws men make? So there was nothing left Monroe and Trudy but to hitch up common-law. Monroe wanted to take her back to Atoka and settle there. He had his eye on a nice enough little spread where they could raise cotton and corn and kids. But the town wouldn't stand for it, even though it wasn't a real, lawful marriage. The people did everything they could to make Monroe and Trudy's life miserable. And I'm sure Mama never let up on them.

So Monroe and Trudy chased up north then, to New York, and that's where they took up residence. I don't think they ever did get married, even up there where they could. Seems like you get started in a certain way, and you just keep going that way. They had three kids, one-two-three like that, a girl and two boys. They called the first-born Blue, after me, even though she was the girl. Trudy sent me pictures, and all of them kids was as cute and smart as they could be.

But Monroe's eyes begun to wander again. As Mama always said about Monroe, "Borned fickle, raised fickle, pickled fickle." And I guess if anyone knowed, Mama knowed. He picked up and left Trudy and the kids and went back on the tracks, so becoming the no-good Mr. Monroe.

Trudy done okay, though. She had inherited her healing hands from her grandfather, and she went about making people well and happy. She come out to California with the kids once to visit me and stayed, oh, a goodly spell and just about turned the town upside down with her healing. But that's another story.

Monroe, he told me on that visit of his, "Blue, I'll never forget Trudy. I owe Trudy my life. And Cully. And you too. But I just had to go. I can't tell you why. The tracks is calling me. The land is calling me. Can't you hear it, Blue? Come with me."

That old devil Monroe. I was living over to Santa Rosa at the time right beside the railroad tracks, and was just putting together money to buy this farm. I hadn't yet met Hannah. And Monroe, he sat there through the night pouring out muscatel for the both of us, waiting for that midnight train whistle to blow and get my blood all hot and rushing, and then he whispered, "Can't you hear the tracks calling you, Blue?" Then he pulled out his French

178

harp and started in playing that damn "Red River Valley" of his. And he said, "Won't you come with me?"

I took me a long minute then. I give it some hard thought. It was like I was trying to remember a lesson I had learned years and years before, a lesson out of that geography I never got. Here I was, what? Nearly thirty, I guess. I had me a few ideas in my head, nothing big, nothing important. I was, as Mama always said, "free, white, and twenty-one." My life was mine. I could do with it what I wanted. And then it come to me, what I was trying to remember. I said — I took Monroe's hand, I remember — and I said, "Oh, I guess not, Monroe."

What I remembered was that boy of eleven, about lost out in Wellaway, Texas, that boy which had done so much living so fast. Monroe was in the shack, laying under Trudy's hand, healing and crazy in love. Black Cully was standing over them. But I was outside by myself, all alone by myself, fidgety and wondering what to do next.

Chicago Stumps was gone. I had thanked him for his help, and asked him where was he heading now. He said back to Downey. I said I was going west to California, and it looked like I was going alone, and didn't he want to come, too. He said what did he want to go to California for. He said Rainbow Red had moved down to the Southern Pacific Line, and he wasn't braving Rainbow Red to ride to California, not for love nor money. I said it was a beautiful land, California was, and it was calling, and didn't he hear it. He said he had business back in Downey.

I felt kindly bumped around. I felt kindly blue. I went over to the train yard and stood among the tracks. Wellaway's a railroad town, a junction where nearly a half-dozen railway lines hook up, and there ain't nothing but tracks and crossties in Wellaway, going off in every direction. It was hot, blistering hot. Rays of heat waved up all around me, so it was hard to see, and everything had a miragey look to it. I stood looking first down one pair of tracks, then the next, then the next, thinking, "Where to? Where to?"

This is the thing about those tracks. On a flatlands — and there ain't none any flatter than Wellaway — that pair of tracks stretches out just forever and always, losing theirselves in the distance, dropping away until the two tracks seem to become just one track, like out there in the future somewhere, they meet. But you know they don't. They never meet.

And if you stand there and look in one direction, then turn and look in the next direction, it don't seem like it makes a bit of difference in the world which way you end up going.

It didn't matter about Monroe. It didn't matter about Marge or Mama or Mrs. Landover. What it come down to in the end was that I looked to the west last. And so that's the way I went.

Rainbow Red, I knowed, was out there ahead of me. Desert. Wild land. And that's another story, too.